Strings

Other poetry collections by Paul B. Janeczko

POETSPEAK: IN THEIR WORK,
    ABOUT THEIR WORK
DONT FORGET TO FLY
POSTCARD POEMS

Strings:
A Gathering of Family Poems

Selected by Paul B. Janeczko

BRADBURY PRESS / SCARSDALE, NEW YORK

Copyright © 1984 by Paul B. Janeczko. Pages 155–161 constitute an extension of the copyright page.

Bradbury Press, Inc.
2 Overhill Road
Scarsdale, N.Y. 10583
An affiliate of Macmillan, Inc.
Collier Macmillan Canada, Inc.
Manufactured in the United States of America
10 9 8 7 6 5 4 3 2 1
The part-title illustration is taken from the jacket by Neil Waldman.
The text of this book is set in 11 pt. Baskerville.
Library of Congress Cataloging in Publication Data
Main entry under title:
Strings: a gathering of family poems.
Includes index. YA
Summary: A collection of 125 poems based on the poets' experiences of family life, as parents, children, brothers and sisters, husbands and wives, cousins, nieces and nephews, and grandchildren.
1. Family—Poetry. 2. American poetry—20th century.
[1. Family life—Poetry. 2. American poetry—Collections]
I. Janeczko, Paul B.
PS595.F34S77   1984   811'.5'080354   83-21564
ISBN 0-02-747790-8

My strings tie gently with love,
firmly with memories to
Jay, who survived a 327–Chevy and Vietnam,
John, who survived the seminary and Korea,
Mark, who survived a Barracuda and law school,
Mary, who survived a bike ride and growing up
    with four older brothers,
my mother, who kept us in kielbasa and cole slaw, and
my father, who has the slides(somewhere)to prove it.

This book is for them.

Contents

Strings:
From Children

Strings:
From Brothers and Sisters

Strings:
From Cousins

Strings:
From Nieces and Nephews

Strings:
From Grandchildren

Strings

The String of My Ancestors

When I need string I can't find it,
but today
string is everywhere.

Shame on the one who
does not want string.

I must not forget my ancestors.
I do up packages:
little gold cars and ivory servants
for their new lives.

I must not forget my children.
I teach them cats' cradles:
Jacob's Ladder, The Bridge and The River,
to keep them out of mischief.

I tie bows on my children's fingers.
They must not forget
their ancestors.

When you cut string
it crawls off
in two directions.

— Nina Nyhart

Strings:
From Wives and Husbands

Surfaces

        darling
you are not at all
like a pool or a rose
my thoughts do not dart in your depths
like cool goldfish
nor does your skin suggest petals
you are not *like* anything (except perhaps
my idea of what you are like

I think you are like
what our children need to grow beautiful
what I need to be most myself)
when the moon comes out I do not think of you
but sometimes you remind me of the moon:
your surfaces are unbelievably real

This is how I feel about you:
suppose
on the surface of a rippling pool
the moon shone clearly reflected
like a yellow rose
then
if a cloud floated over it
        I would hate the sky

— *Peter Meinke*

Ten Week Wife

Dried to a pit of meanness,
talking to nobody, looking

out from the wrong side of my face,
I was a salt flat, a dug

out road bed, six feet of wasp
and a worse sting coming,

a sucked egg, a picked chicken,
a doll wound up and run

down, been everywhere,
done by everybody.

Then you eased in,
squeezed in, thumping

new life, plumping me.
Now I am a Toby jug,

round and sassy, sleek and smooth
and puffed up full of you,

my old frame fleshed out,
sod breaking to bloom,

salt gone sweet, wasp unstung,
a laid egg, a done doll

picked up and planted,
making roots, driving them deep,

growing smug, feeling like
a balloon in a world with no pins.

— *Rhoda Donovan*

Sounding

—for Judy

I envy the silence
Of the sounding stone:
The straight line of its descent
Creates a circle that grows
Until it rings the lake
And escapes in sighs on the shore.
Sounding the depths,
It speaks the water's
One true name.

I wish I could sound my love for you
In a poem so perfectly silent
It would say everything.
Each poem descends
And descends
While I remain at the surface,
Letting out more and more line,
Waiting for the quiver
Of the rope going slack
As the poem touches bottom.

I wait, I let out all of the line,
But still I find no bottom.

—David Jauss

Washing Windows

All day we make our clockwise circle around the house,
you on the inside, me on the out,
going through the motions, the awkward ballet
                          of some purgatorial experiment,

our polishings the matched waves,
                          one pressed against the other,
nodding, tapping, rubbing out this streak and that.
What is that you're saying? mine or yours?

I shout trying to remember what I did at the party last night.
Did you really do your kickup dance from the *West Side Story*
and did I, late, whirl around with a lamp shade on my head,
arms out in hilarious mockery of the cliché and myself?

Nevertheless finally it's done, and having spent
just a few hours from our lives we're back
to where we started, grinning at one another, at our prospect:

to sit inside for one moment of the year purged at last,
completely sober, watching the wind outside,
that vagrant never so transparent staggering around the
     neighborhood.

— *Peter Wild*

On the Eve of Our Anniversary

Spring approaches   blowing east
     from Minnesota   still   drifting snow.
Fields   recently black   with birds

mound   in rows of wind.
Tonight   housebound   you baby
   our plants   spread paper
dump pots   exposing   the married roots.
   Purple shade   of the passion leaf.
Pale stems   of coleus.
   Strands   of spider shoots.
The dog stretches   beside you   noses
   into the damp dirt   sniffing for something
like herself.   She finds   your hand.
   You hold   a baby tears.
I admire each heart   each head-shaped leaf
   even   its miniature   milkweed flower
barely   there   a fairy hand   you insist I see
   and touch.   Dear   this March   as snow
comes and goes   as we pair   wedding ourselves
   again   pray   these roots too   outgrow their pots
yet growing   still   the wind will keep us in
   to trim   and feed
this spring   these plants   our rings.

— *Gary Margolis*

How About

the green screen door
that slammed shut
hard
every time
Bert came in
from the field

how about all the times
Mable had to prop
that heavy door
open
with her foot
as she tossed out
the dirty dishwater

and how about that torn
kitchen linoleum
she'd wanted
replaced

and how about the cobs
she hauled in
for her old cookstove
years after all the neighbors
had gas ranges

and how about the tin tub
she had to bathe in
in the pantry

and how about the piles
and piles and
piles of Kansas City Stars
Bert saved for years
just in case he ever
learned to read

and how about those chickens
Bert kept in the house
so the coyotes wouldn't
get them

how about that poor woman

they say she went crazy
stark raving mad
from the chicken shit
gumming the keys
of her baby grand

—*Sheryl L. Nelms*

One of the Boys

Wanting to lie down on a bed
to read a book,
I am drawn not to the usual
marriage-bed but to the
lower bunk in my sons' room.

I lie down where Austin lies
each night, a seven-year-old
starting fresh, who has not unlearned
weeping at hurt, nor unlearned
the wild gesture that is like
the flash of an animal
escaping into the woods.

This is the male room,
where the mail of my life
has been piling up, unopened, for years.
I want to read it now
as I bask here in the exclusion
of all wives, mothers, daughters, even
lovers, even
the very best of witches.

A week ago I shared the room
of our car with my wife
as she drove us for the first time
to a marriage counselor. How far apart
two people in a car can be!
A glassy cave, and two
prototypes of the human
staring straight ahead
at the centuries-long task
of learning how to speak.
I wept then to think of Emmett,
whose dreams each night
are clouds moving like prophecies
across Austin's sky.

Now I fly in this lower bunk
into the future, the pilot
not to be seen
but believed, and felt
all around me in the form
of a magic circle,
a space the wizard carries
at all times inside him,
its power the source of any feat,
including the amazing
dissolution of walls between rooms.

— *Philip Dacey*

Trying

He has, by his wife's reckoning, failed so often,
He thinks failure is just trying, so the cat's
Got his daughter's love, the car his son's reverence,
And birds beat and rob him in his own garden,
Leaving him for caterpillars and aphids to peck at.

But each afternoon he raises his hose again
And out of it leaps a sweet unstinting jet
Whose shed plumes of spray, mixing with sun,
Unfurl a rainbow so dim and delicate
No one but him can see the good he's done.

— Leonard Nathan

Strings:
From Parents

Birth

In the steel room
where one becomes two
we were delivered.
But for a moment
I saw the rope
blue, shiny between us;
then it was cut
tied without pain
being heartbeat and no nerve.

As you wailed in your heated bed
a nurse held the pan so I could see
that valentine we all arrive with,
that red pad of which you were the lily
with the cord lying bleached across it
like a root pulled from the water
like a heartroot torn free.

— George Ella Lyon

For My Son, Born During an Ice Storm

Steven, your birth brought
Such a storm of joy
I had to sit down in the Delivery Room
And hold my head.

That day, even the lilacs
Were borne down
By the diamonds on their backs.

— David Jauss

The New Mothers

Nearly seven,
walls loosen, it's already dark,
dinner trays rattle by,
nurses slack off, catch
a smoke, let go.
Roses bloom in every room.

Nearby
the egg-bald babies lie, stretching
pink like rows of knitting,
insects in cases, and cry
tiny metal tunes,
hairpins scratching
sky.

The mothers gather
together in clutches
of happy nylon,
brushing and brushing their hair.

They bunch at the frosted windows
in quilted trios
watching the parking lot where

pair after pair
the yellow headlights arc
through blowing snow —
the fathers
        are coming

— *Carol Shields*

:.

Catechisms:
Talking with a Four-Year-Old

What's the oldest thing that's living?
> Trees probably—California redwoods.
I mean that moves around.
> A tortoise I guess.
No, I mean that moves around and talks:
the oldest thing.
> Some person somewhere.

Are your bones going to come through?
> What?
When your sunburn peels, are your bones
going to poke through?
> No, no, there's new skin under there.
> It's tough.
Will they ever?
> Not unless I get a bad break.
Don't do that.
> No.
They'd have to put you in the hard stuff.
> What?
The white bone stuff. They'd have to put it
all over.
> That's called a cast.
Do they sew bones?
> No, bones can grow back together—
Who will die first?

—George Ella Lyon

Poop

my daughter, blake, is in kindergarten.
they are teaching her to be a docile citizen
and, incidentally, to read.
concurrently, like many of us,
she has become a trifle anal compulsive.
complications ensue.

i ask her what she has learned today.
she says, "i learned the pledge of allegiance."
"how does it go?" i ask.
"it goes," she says, "i poop allegiance
to the poop of the united poops of ameripoop."

"that's good," i say, "that's very good. what else?"
"o say can you poop, by the dawn's early poop,
what so proudly we pooped . . ."

for christmas, she improvises,
"away in a pooper, all covered with poop,
the little lord poopus
lay pooping his poop."

she has personalized other traditional favorites
as well. someone tried to teach her the "our father."
her version goes, "our pooper, who art in poopland,
hallowed be thy poop. thy poopdom poop,
thy poop be pooped, on earth as it is in poopland."

surely hemingway would feel one-upped.
surely the second pooping is at hand.

a fortune teller told us blake would be
our greatest sorrow and our greatest joy.
already it is true.

— *Gerald Locklin*

Portrait

A child draws the outline of a body.
She draws what she can, but it is white all through,
she cannot fill in what she knows is there.
Within the unsupported line, she knows
that life is missing; she has cut
one background from another. Like a child,
she turns to her mother.

And you draw the heart
against the emptiness she has created.

— *Louise Glück*

Smell My Fingers

— for Jessica

Smell my fingers my daughter
says and thrusts them
at my nose. I back dive off
my chair as if the air were
poisoned. Where have they been
those sweaty things with six

years of sticky places
scenting their past? She laughs
and chases me around the room
with germicidal weapons,
insists on my surrender.
Caught, I find a pine cone
in her fist. She tells me
it is spring and that means perfume.

— David B. Axelrod

: :

Buying the Dog

He's shy Buck McLeish says
stops spray painting the John Deere
stepping out the dark oil smell barn
through a brief patch of Lindsay Ontario sun
and into the mellow light of the kennels

where the dog who has been
in a religious fit of silence
since birth   stands
petrified in his corner.
The other dogs wave their bodies against the fence.
Buck gives us the character of each hound—
he's mental   he's savage
and this one
the one he's going to sell us
is shy.

In the car through all the small towns
Omemee   Fowler's Corners   Jermyn
the dog buries his head in the backseat
for 115 miles the wide eyes
stare into car leather.
Towns the history of his bones
Preneven   Marmora   Actinolite   Enterprise

Bellrock and home.

Carefully
the dog puts his feet
like thin white sticks out of the car and
takes off JESUS
like a dolphin
over the fields for all we know
he won't be coming back—

—Michael Ondaatje

Murgatroyd

Whenever we would open, there he stood,
With the supreme authority of need:
The face with pansy markings, eyes alight;
The body young, as meager as a bird's
Under the lusterless neglected fur.

Our cat confronted him, the Amazon,
Disdainful princess, nourished and secure,
Swinging her paw at the intruder there;
He quivered, but continued hovering
As if it were impossible to fail.

Our guilt, intolerable, weighed us down:
After three days, a saucerful of milk;
Complete capitulation, gates ajar
To grooming and a cushion and our love.
These were his right; he never questioned it.

—Celeste Turner Wright

Shaggy Dog Story

We're rolling on the living room floor
his teeth lightly holding my wrist.
Vowels come through them
warming my sleeve. I'm the more breathless
because he smokes less. I look
at his magician's face
in a kind of sleep
wag what's left of my tail, and we
roll for a new view.

— *Frank Steele*

: :

First Surf

A little sparrow
attempting his
first surf
dipped by my car's nose
into the air wave,
but dipped too low.
I saw the life clump,
a throbbing rock,
from my rearview mirror,
and thought of stopping.
But drove on home,
fearful for my children.

— *Emanuel Di Pasquale*

To My Children, Fearing for Them

Terrors are to come. The earth
is poisoned with narrow lives.
I think of you. What you will

live through, or perish by, eats
at my heart. What have I done? I
need better answers than there are

to the pain of coming to see
what was done in blindness,
loving what I cannot save. Nor,

your eyes turning toward me,
can I wish your lives unmade
though the pain of them is on me.

— *Wendell Berry*

Poem of the Mother

The heart goes out ahead
scouting for him
while I stay at home
keeping the fire,
holding the house down
around myself
like a skirt from the high wind.

The boy does not know
how my eye strains to make out
his small animal shape
swimming hard across the future
nor that I have strengthened myself
like the wood side of this house
for his benefit.

I stay still
so he can rail against me.
I stay at the fixed center of things
like a jar on its shelf
or the clock on the mantel
so when his time comes
he can leave me.

— *Myra Sklarew*

For My Daughter

This is the summer storm,
soft rain and the dark,
the long lightning you murmur against
sleeping on the porch.
I carry you away from it,
sleeping, to your room.

And these are the steps of forgetfulness,
of leaving pain:
may honesty, the plain monkey
with a lost eye, never leave you;
may you have lovers numerous
as cardinals in the hemlock.
May they return forever.
May you hate fashion,
have the beauty of the potter's hands,
work in communities of friends.
And Whitman carried from the wreck
of my childhood:
"stand up for the poor
and the weak and the crazy."

These are the steps to the room
where parents are forgotten.
Because we die I think
of the story of grass
that has lived forever
waving swords that can be cut
but come back and advance.

Because like any child
you sleep in the shell of the future

I stand with fists clenched, as rain
carries the sounds of your breathing away.

— *Ed Ochester*

Business as Usual

Under the dining room light
the old conspiracy flickers:
who failed the checkbook this time,
who hid the newspaper, tipped the ashtray,
left windows open in the rain . . .

The children are upstairs in bed
listening to the grass growing —
it's simple now, in moonlight.
All day they have been speaking to
Mr. South Wind, asking favors:
blow away the neighbors
in their lawnchairs, bring
some new friends in a balloon.

But fathers are useful, too.
I'm required to teach them how to spell
so they can write their dreams,
required to learn a magic chant
to make tornadoes go away,
to tame a big bull cat for them,
and watch their hands, and sing.

And since I cannot fix the tv set
or the ugly eye of a ceiling leak,
cannot make the insects stop

squashing themselves against the screens,
since I am not on speaking terms with
the south wind, or the cupboard crickets,
or even the column of figures
I helped to invent,

it's really the least I can do

here beside the window
and a whole army of health grass
growing greener
growing loud
in the last lovely light
of the moon, the moon, the moon.

—Mark Vinz

Afternoon

My mouse, my girl in gray, I speak to her;
One day in autumn I will wander through
A closed amusement park, past shacks that were
A moment since the palaces of rue
Where gaudy prizes hung along the stand
Seduced the quarter from no gambler's hand.

And there will be the boarded House of Fun,
And leaves will tumble past the Whirl-O-Ride.
I will move on, content as anyone,
And then will see her walking to my side,
My mouse, my girl. She will not speak, but smile,
And we will walk together, for a while.

—Donald Hall

For My Daughter

She often lies with her hands behind her head
in a San Quentin pose, arms forming a pair
of small empty wings.

She does not slip from the bath in a loose
towel, affording Follies' glimpses
of rump and thigh. She does lumber by
in a robe of immense dunciness.

Her dates are fixed up or blind
often, like specimens, behind thick glass.
She leaves late, returns by 12:00 afraid
perhaps that she will turn into
something worse.

She comes to me and wants to know what to do.
I say I do not know.
She comes to me and wants to know if it will
ever be alright.
I say yes but it will take a long time.

— *Ronald Koertge*

Commencement, Pingree School

Among these North Shore tennis tans I sit,
In seersucker dressed, in small things fit;
Within a lovely tent of white I wait
To see my lovely daughter graduate.

Slim boughs of blossom tap the tent and stamp
　　Their shadows like a bower on the cloth.
The birds in twos glide down the grassy ramp
　　To graduation's candle, moth and moth.

The Master makes his harrumphs. Music. Prayer.
　　Demure and close in rows, the seniors sway.
Class loyalty solidifies the air.
　　At every name, a body wends her way

Through greenhouse shade and rustle to receive
A paper of divorce and endless leave.
As each accepts her scroll of rhetoric,
Up pops a Daddy with a Nikon. *Click.*

—John Updike

:.:

The Writer

In her room at the prow of the house
Where light breaks, and the windows are tossed with linden,
My daughter is writing a story.

I pause in the stairwell, hearing
From her shut door a commotion of typewriter-keys
Like a chain hauled over a gunwale.

Young as she is, the stuff
Of her life is a great cargo, and some of it heavy:
I wish her a lucky passage.

But now it is she who pauses,
As if to reject my thought and its easy figure.
A stillness greatens, in which

The whole house seems to be thinking,
And then she is at it again with a bunched clamor
Of strokes, and again is silent.

I remember the dazed starling
Which was trapped in that very room, two years ago;
How we stole in, lifted a sash

And retreated, not to affright it;
And how for a helpless hour, through the crack of the door,
We watched the sleek, wild, dark

And iridescent creature
Batter against the brilliance, drop like a glove
To the hard floor, or the desk-top,

And wait then, humped and bloody,
For the wits to try it again; and how our spirits
Rose when, suddenly sure,

It lifted off from a chair-back,
Beating a smooth course for the right window
And clearing the sill of the world.

It is always a matter, my darling,
Of life or death, as I had forgotten. I wish
What I wished you before, but harder.

— *Richard Wilbur*

Missing My Daughter

This wall-paper has lines that rise
Upright like bars, and overhead,
The ceiling's patterned with red roses.
On the wall opposite the bed
The staring looking-glass encloses
Six roses in its white of eyes.

Here at my desk, with note-book open
Missing my daughter, makes those bars
Draw their lines upward through my mind.
This blank page stares at me like glass
Where stared-at roses wish to pass
Through petalling of my pen.

An hour ago, there came an image
Of a beast that pressed its muzzle
Between bars. Next, through tick and tock

Of the reiterating clock
A second glared with the wide dazzle
Of deserts. The door, in a green mirage,

Opened. In my daughter came.
Her eyes were wide as those she has,
The round gaze of her childhood was
White as the distance in the glass
Or on a white page, a white poem.
The roses raced around her name.

— Stephen Spender

Now That Your Shoulders Reach My Shoulders

My shoulders once were yours for riding.
My feet were yours for walking, wading.
My morning once was yours for taking.

Still I can almost feel the pressure
Of your warm hands clasping my forehead
While my hands grasped your willing ankles.

Now that your shoulders reach my shoulders
What is there left for me to give you?
Where is a weight to lift as welcome?

— Robert Francis

Why I Never Went into Politics

—for Brad

my son
I promised you a world and see
it is all gone it is beyond
repairing we must learn
to live without it

each day a parade of soldiers
goes past followed by dogs
whose clinking tags proclaim
they have owners
and they are not mad

we are told not to look up or down
the sky is not public the earth
is not ours
we are told to look
straight ahead and march forward
and kill
that is the way it is done
in this land

my son
I love you and having told you
all I remember all that is left
of an old story
I tell you that those
who use the language of poets
are poets and those
who use the language of thieves
are thieves

—*Richard Shelton*

Last Born

Drunk,
you move
unsteadily
in the dark,
testing
your steps
on the kitchen floor
where you first
learned to walk
as I watched you.

—Judith Kirkwood

Subway Psalm

It's the first storm of the winter
and the worst since 1888,
the girl on television said.

I keep slipping in my leather-soled shoes.
Twice I've turned into a windmill
in my efforts to keep from falling.

At the top of the stairs leading down
to the subway, Johnnie watches me,
not just with his eyes but with his arms and legs.
He'll do his best to save the old man.

That's how I must have looked at him
when he was five or six years old.
Now he's twenty-six, and it seems
we've traded places.

Why are you laughing?
he asks me.
The honest answer is:
Because you look so funny, standing there
like that, my beautiful son,
and because I've loved you
for such a long time and because this
is the finest storm I've ever seen
and everything is exactly as it should be.

—Alden Nowlan

Widow to Her Son

I have taken up the dulcimer again.
I did not believe the songs would come back
from so far, but they did.
"Old Grey Goose" was easy,
and the other joysome songs.
I remember when your pa first came courting
and we sat in the parlor
with the double dulcimer between us
and rubbed knees. The light
from a coal oil lamp was small,
but he was Jesus' own handsome man,
and he taught me river runs,
how to fret and feather the dark poplar
into sweet freshets of song.
Told me, knowing ma and daddy
were in the kitchen listening
for both sets of strings,
that a split quill caught
off an angel's wing makes the best pick,
and a dog's rib bone the best noter.

He was a caution, and I reckoned
we'd be married directly, and we were.
I never thought these tunes would be so easy
to find after all these years alone,
and how far away they feel,
hearing them on the one set of strings,
since my shadow couldn't catch a tune
if it had handles on it.
Listen. You can hear the river rising.

—*R. T. Smith*

:.

Missing the Children

Yesterday my children left for college,
I exhausted myself with garden work.
Today I wake up feeling gnawed and sore
And think of the baby cardinal,
Feathers askew, unwieldy in innocence,
It had fallen into my mulch hole
And I sought to help by lifting
It out on the tip of my shovel.
Promptly it ran from me into
The dog pen where it was mauled.
I sat on a stump and breathed hard
While its mother circled and shrieked.
She spent the whole day calling
And searching for her child.

I wish I had been born less clumsy
To this world and grown
In my love more naturally.
I think of my cabin so far away.
Because of spring it is trying
To become a poem. I feel it rise
Lightly on ferns that tilt it to the sun.
Around it saplings lift their leaves
Into the canopy of my brain. If I were
There I would thin them like a harsh god,
Arranging sky between their trunks.
The cabin is sweetened by cardinal's song.
As it unbinds from winter, groans and sighs
Upon its footers, it wonders, where is Zimmer?
But I am far away, searching the rooms
Of my house, looking for my children.

— *Paul Zimmer*

Reflexes

There was a powder the druggist had—
used it on my hand when I squeezed
a glass ornament at Christmas: I
picked it up, held it up and held it tighter,
three stages I can still distinguish.
Then I was holding a handful of blood.

This man's oldest daughter died
from a dormitory fire—famous at the time.
She got out, then went back.
She lay for days in the burn ward.
She had been skinned alive. No chance.
Her father, the pharmacist, understood.

Sometimes, you have to imagine the worst
to prepare: the calm fire drill at school,
or the desperate decisions that come
in the dark: which room, which child?
We fuzz it up with heroics, charades.
No one can picture the worst.

—Marvin Bell

Strings:
From Children

The Field

The breeze stops, the afternoon heat rises,
and she hears his back porch screen door slap shut.
She sits still, lets her mind follow him through
the swinging gate into the field, his shirt
and white flannel pants freshly pressed, his new
racquet held so loosely that it balances
exactly in his hand. Now my father
takes the stile in two steps. And now my mother
turns in the lawn chair, allows herself the sight
of him lifting the racquet as if to
keep it dry. This instant, before he comes
to where she sits under the trees, these two
can choose whatever lives they want, but from
the next it is fixed in shadow and light.

— *David Huddle*

:.

Mothers

—for J. B.

Oh mother,
here in your lap,
as good as a bowlful of clouds,
I your greedy child
am given your breast,
the sea wrapped in skin,
and your arms,
roots covered with moss
and with new shoots sticking out
to tickle the laugh out of me.
Yes, I am wedded to my teddy
but he has the smell of you
as well as the smell of me.
Your necklace that I finger
is all angel eyes.
Your rings that sparkle
are like the moon on the pond.
Your legs that bounce me up and down,
your dear nylon-covered legs,
are the horses I will ride
into eternity.

Oh mother,
after this lap of childhood
I will never go forth
into the big people's world
as an alien,
a fabrication,
or falter
when someone else
is as empty as a shoe.

—*Anne Sexton*

Nightmare

Expecting to be put in a sack and dumped in a ditch,
sister and brother fled
but were imprisoned by a witch
in a haunted wood
where dark trees grew tightly round
and in the middle a tower stood,
and when night came and animals sprang,
legs rooted to earth and could not flee . . .

I was firmly convinced that if I ran away
nobody anywhere wanted me.

— *Edward Field*

I Was the Child

I was the child
daughter of the waves,
swimming first in innocent
baby puddles hovering round my Mother's breasts;
but reaching always, hand over chubby hand
to the sunny naked waters;
the lake of my being.

Mother, you let me run
and splash —
soft baby skin wide to the sun
shine and knowing,
not knowing, cradled me
from warm sand castles
washed by fickle waves,

to the shallow field of water, then
to the weedy depths
of my lake.

How does it feel, I wonder
(I can not know, not yet)
to watch your own flesh crawl, walk
and swim from the womb, and still
somehow, love each growing step?
Mother, did you feel your heart
contract, as willingly,
you offered me to the waves?
Did your bottled voice long to burst
crying out:

> Oh my Sunshine!
> My last blond bubbly
> Sunshine girl—
> Stay here forever by my side!

Because I have felt that longing
in you, have heard
the quieted cry stifle all
but the desperate emptiness
in your eyes;
I can hear as if you speak:

> Oh my Daughter
> Child of the waves
> My Flower, My Weed,
> If you must go, go ever so slowly
> Into that dark rippled sunshine lake!

— *Valerie S. Warren*

: :

Hunting at Dusk

—for Dennis Sampson

Before father shot the moon out
with his .22 scoped rifle,
he picked three legs off a
jackrabbit on the run.

The creature rose
from the earth
with each shot
of propelled gravity

using its muzzle as a hoof
and one paw
to bound off into
the corn stubble bleeding.

And we just all cheered from the car;
our uncles and my father getting high
off beer, getting cocky—that's when he
shot the moon out; being no game warden,

they started naming stars. He shot holes
in both dippers, shot several cows
out of the Milky Way, one elephant,
and picked a crab off Hercules.

I hit the shit-list that night
when I yelled out something
about waking up tomorrow
and shooting out the sun.

—Doug Cockrell

Two Hopper

Dad he said the White Sox
couldn't lose
as long as his old
sky blue ice box filled with Hamms
was running smoothly.

Dad he said the White Sox
shouldn't fear
because that bastard
Eddie Robinson could hit the ball
from here to Hades.

Dad was also fond of saying
up the middle where it counts
at second short and center
if you got the strength
you shouldn't sweat the Yankees
or the friggin' Indians.

If memory's correct
the Yankees *always* came in
first the Cleveland delegation
always came in second we
were *always* sloppy thirds.

My Dad he said a lot of things
you wouldn't tell your Mother.

— Ron Ikan

Pa

When we got home, there was our Old Man
hanging just by his hands from the windmill vane,
forty feet off the ground, his pants down,
inside out, caught on his shoes — he never wore
underwear in summer — shirt tail flapping,
hair flying.

My brother grabbed a board.
We lugged it up the windmill and ran it out
like a diving board under The Old Man's feet
and wedged our end below a crossbar. The Old Man
kept explaining, "I climbed up to oil a squeak,
reached out to push the vane around, slipped, damn
puff of wind, I swung right out."

We felt strange helping him down.
In our whole lives, we never really held him before,
and now with his pants tangled around his feet
and him talking faster, getting hoarser all the way
down, explaining, explaining.

On solid ground, he quivered, pulling up his pants.
I said, "Good thing we came when we did." His eyes
burned from way back. His hands
were like little black claws. He spit Copenhagen
and words almost together: "Could have hung on
a long time yet. Anyway, you should have been home
half an hour ago."

— Leo Dangel

In White Tie

In white tie
and tails my father
danced the first two
times in his life, first
with my bride and then with
her mother. There were close
to 300 people watching, and he
kept a smile on his face, got
through it just fine. I felt
like kissing him because I'd
been through enough of a
war to know courage
when I saw it.

— *David Huddle*

The River

— for Dutch Welch

Winter,
late afternoon
the sun a pale flare
in the westering trees.

Here, the willows
have almost gone home
to the dark,
there is a perceptible
wind trailing the edges
of minutes.

This afternoon
it was warm.

And now my father
picking up decoys swings
lead weights around their necks,
his back to the west.

All day
having moved in this river
like a pleasant doom,
his surgeries blending
with the buckbrush and trees,
he has had his eyes
unraveled by birds.

Tonight the deer
will unfold themselves from the dark
and come forth.

In the deepest channels
slush ice will form itself
in cold lacy jags,
the slews grow brittle
with ice.

I look west.

There is a single hole
in the clouds through which
time is escaping.

—*Don Welch*

Rowing

Early Saturdays
father and I argued to the lake,
oars strapped in a V
to the Chrysler.

He insisted I feather them,
roll my wrists so the oars
cut air with least resistance,
enter water without sound.
No good. My left arm weak
I pulled in circles.
We shifted seats and he rowed
ruler-straight.

Because we spoke by shouting
I tasted my hands' blood
on a college crew
snowy Aprils
as the coach stood silent
and huge in furs,
superior as a yacht
as we slid and grunted past.

One summer
I drove father to the lake
bitter from old failures
and rowed — contemptuous, nervous —
oars skipping despite my skill.
It was an invitation to conversation,
the stiff locks squeaking
"I love   I love."

— *Ed Ochester*

∴

Clay and Water

In my father's brickyard
I saw walls of brick around me. Bricks
Bricks, so bright they were,
One piled upon the other
Like small red suitcases left in the Gare St. Lazare.

I stood in my father's brickyard
And I wondered where I came from, or if
There was something I could ask him,
Something that we would not stumble on.
— Climbed to my father's office.
Covered with white dust, there were files,
And a desk — and there! My father, curious
As I to know why I had come.
Then I asked him, "Tell me about bricks,"
Thinking that he certainly
Had something about bricks to tell me.
"What is there to tell?" — "About bricks,"
I insisted, "about their names."
He looked through
Papers on his desk, all disarranged,
And asked Mr. Bard, his partner, who
Didn't know; and finding nothing to tell,
He said, "Bricks come from clay and water.
They come from water and clay."

Later, when I walked into the yard,
I looked up and saw my father waving at me,
Standing like an old man
Cemented in the strong window.

— *Sandra Hochman*

He

has never written me a letter himself.
Or called.

My mother dials and says,
"Here he is."

— *Ronald Koertge*

Sum

My accountant father
counts pebbles and lawn-
mowers and edges the grasses
with somber precision.
His life like machine tape
droops down in a white beard
and ends in a darkness
of double red figures
which mount like a staircase
toward some *ergo sum*.

With asterisk eyes braced
he dreams of a golf score.
Report cards and budgets
are good things to sleep on
except that they flutter
and need constant folding.
Calendrical suns stand
like forms left to fill in
as he considers the number
of hamburger patties still
stacked in the freezer.

My accountant father
made me count
one day to two
and I never made it through.

My accountant father
confides in his mother
that he really has nothing.
She calls up to ask us
about what he tells her:
we place all his things all
around where he'll be sure
to see them and count them
and sit waiting in three's.
We're all we can gather.

My accountant father
lies counting to sixty
and counting in two's
to fill up the nothing
of the second hand's shadow.

My daddy. Accounted.
A hand full of pebbles.
He never was married,
divided or touched.

—*James Nolan*

: :

Stepfather: A Girl's Song

Again heavy rain drives him home.
It follows him from the cornfield
washing away footsteps, covering tracks.
For years his eyes undressed me.
There's a river in his stance
sweeping me away.

He comes into my bedroom
around corners of moonlight.
Unexpected, he catches me
in his big arms. An ancient music
at the edge of my mouth.
He looks at me slantwise, warns:
"These hands whipped a mule crazy
& killed a man in '63. They
remember a bird's clear touch."

My hands are sparrows, stars
caught in tangled dance of bowed
branches. An undertow
drags me down.
His mouth on mine,
kissing my mama.

— *Yusef Komunyakaa*

Open Roads

My stepfather was a hobo because he didn't know any better.
He appeared out of nowhere when I was nine, broke,
looking for work; half an hour later the police appeared
to question him briefly about the theft of a diamond ring.

Actually he wasn't a real hobo; he was more of a thief.
Real hobos are middle-class lawyers who give up their practice
to follow the open highways with battered gym bags.
My stepfather collapsed on the livingroom sofa and felt at home.
He had never seen a real livingroom before. He liked it.
Dark polished furniture and real silver in drawers.
My mother liked him because he was cheerful
    and easy to understand.
My father was in the hospital in London reading Juvenal.
A woman alone with a large house and two children
    may like anyone.
He'd been in Kingston once, which is big time, sophisticated,
but he never talked about Kingston or the small ones either.
When I look back I associate him with lunch bars
    and Woolworths
and park benches and supermarkets and second-hand appliances.
He liked appliances and had a favorite hook on them:
buy a new fridge on credit: sell it for approximately half:
then buy a replacement second-hand: keep the difference.
He liked action and thought it was a good way
    of making money.
He liked used cars a lot: we bought a second-hand truck
when I was ten and worked the country-side with it in summer;
old mattresses, plow points, baling wire, batteries, scrap;
a cast-iron bell from an abandoned farm-house, odd locks,
harness pieces, a black pot that we kept for home;
there's a large difference between scrap and found objects:
it's the same as the difference between garbage and a museum.
Actually he didn't admire hobos; he looked down on them.
My father may have admired the hobos who slept
under bridges in photographs of Paris in the 1920's.
He was an entrepreneur but not to be confused with Edison.
I associated him with gangsters because he wore fedoras
but apart from the occasional beverage room fight
    he wasn't a gangster.

The truck is what remains viable out of this:
a ½-ton green Ford pick-up with a V-8 engine; the truck
remains as a symbol of highways and negotiations,
of pulling into small farm-yards at nine in the morning
and sloshing through mud on the way down to the barn
with a farmer vaguely interested in selling an old thresher
he'd pushed away four years ago; the fields of childhood
remain and the roads remain and the gumshoe boots
   and the equipment
and the barns remain; the sky and the trees are fairly clear
and the truck remains as a way of moving among nature
and people at the same time; of people in the fact of nature
and of art in the fact of junk; the truck was beautiful
and what made it possible: the truck
was what I missed most when I came to the city of light.

— *David Donnell*

∵∴

A Letter from Home

She sends me news of bluejays, frost,
Of stars and now the harvest moon
That rides above the stricken hills.
Lightly, she speaks of cold, of pain,
And lists what is already lost.
Here where my life seems hard and slow,
I read of glowing melons piled
Beside the door, and baskets filled
With fennel, rosemary and dill,
While all she could not gather in
Or hide in leaves, grows black and falls.
Here where my life seems hard and strange,
I read her wild excitement when
Stars climb, frost comes, and bluejays sing.
The broken years will make no change
Upon her wise and whirling heart; —
She knows how people always plan
To live their lives, and never do.
She will not tell me if she cries.

I touch the crosses by her name;
I fold the pages as I rise,
And tip the envelope, from which
Drift scraps of borage, woodbine, rue.

—*Mary Oliver*

Poem for My Mother

Remember when I draped
the ruffled cotton cape
around your shoulders,
turned off the lights
and stood behind your chair,
brushing, brushing your hair.

The friction of the brush
in the dry air
of that small inland town
created stars that flew
as if God himself was there
in the small space
between my hand and your hair.

Now we live on separate coasts
of a foreign country.
A continent stretches between us.
You write of your illness,
your fear of blindness.
You say you wake afraid
to open your eyes.

Mother, if some morning
you open your eyes to see
daylight as a dark room around you,
I will drape a ruffled cotton cape
around your shoulders
and stand behind your chair,
brushing the stars out of your hair.

—*Siv Cedering*

A Common Light

—for my father

That which I should have done
I did not do. Here on the porch
The beginning of spring
Or end of winter
Reflects off the screen. I stare at you
Who now can barely see
Even the light that sparks
The tunnels of dust,
The dust settling
On your shoulder. I used to think
Blindness made a person solitary
And close to God. I watch you shrink
From what you cannot see—
Which should make me scared of age,
But there's a beauty to it
Beyond your resignation. You lay your hand
in shadow on the table
Between us.

On this our annual visit
We will talk to each other,
I to tell you what I've done
And you to comment on it.
There are no children
to distract us
From our purpose. At thirty-seven
You'd already had two sons.
I think you wanted none,
Knowing in that small well of wisdom we deny
That you had no patience, only
The kind of love
That flickers in this common light,

A source of pride
And sorrow. It's a letter you wrote
Years ago and could not finish.

                      Your words

Got away. Your wish
Was small and serious:
That I become, like you, a man of business.
The small love you had
For where words come from, where they go,
Has enlarged in me, my livelihood. That
Which I should have done
I could not do. I rose each morning,
Slack, ingenuous, unreasoning:
I meant to bloom for you,
Tender to all living things.
I forget, each morning, to resume. That which I
Felt to be simple —
To go out among men
And to return a man, solitary, to my room —
Turned out to be complicated.
Childless, without theories or fortunes
To offer, I offer some words. I'd like
To offer myself, to pester your sleeve.
I play with my fork and knife.
I slice an apple for us.

— Steve Orlen

For My Father on His Birthday

Fully imagined, I suppose,
You would be what you are, a tool maker
With a long life of making good tools,
A lonely man, cheated by the circumstances

Which made you deaf.
With a better mind than mine to think you,
Perhaps your boyhood would take shape,
To show you shading out of it,
Some things coming to nothing,
Others making the fence you live behind.
You could then say what you are,
And I, luckier than I have been, agree.

But when I think of you, so often now,
I can only hope you well,
In spite of how things went,
Turned out so badly, the house split up,
My brother so strangely strong so young,
My mother by herself.

Perhaps you are the cause of other ends
As well. My thanks to you, I think,
For helping me decide
Not to stick myself in mill towns all my life.
Your example healed me,
Sent me toward myself and here, to this page,
To try to trap the fleeting things
You showed me

If any of us live at all
Or are designed to think things through,
I would want you thought out once,
And then forgotten, so that I could come back
To rediscover you.
With luck, we have years left,
Years to do the things we want to do,
To be the things we are.

— *Greg Kuzma*

. .
. .

Kitchen Tables

There were two, small one replacing large one
after Charles and I went to Charlottesville
and left them having meals with only three
to sit down, or sometimes just two because Bill,
with Jim Pope, was out courting catastrophe
in their Dodge or the Popes' Ford, oblivion
turned up high on the radio, Pabst cans
cooling their thighs, both those boys in the trance
of a warm summer night when you're able
— our parents had one daughter who died, three
sons who were always leaving for somewhere —
to race toward some girl's house on county
roads that billow up dust behind you while your
mother and father sit at a small, round table.

— *David Huddle*

We Interrupt This Broadcast

They're still my grown-ups
and it's still Sunday afternoon
beneath the table.

It's raining blackjack
but my oak protects me
from the Plock! "Hit me!" Plock!

Motionless, I scurry
in and out of their talk,
hauling back huge wisdoms.

A miscarriage is messy
and I think it has
high, wobbly wheels.

Time and a half
needs a fatter clock.
"Hit me!" Plock! "Too hard!" Laugh.

War is coming but not yet.
There's still half a jug
of sour honey-colored beer

and mother just lit a cigarette.
Hitler could kill me
but he'd have to fight

Roosevelt, Joe Louis
and Daddy to get into the house.
Anyway, I'm a mouse.

—*Judith Hemschemeyer*

Around the Kitchen Table

Around the kitchen table we are never out
of shape, grinning back the skinned and bleeding
shins we picked up in our first front yards,
remembering the black and blue, the sweaty
run-ins with the nuns who always had our number,
recalling how we counted time by cornsilk
curling from our burning corners,
by the hams and sausage Grandpa strung
around the smokehouse, by the smelt

we shoveled in the car and drove all night with,
breathing stars and silos, breathing whispers
in the scarves the girls gave us, counting time
by frost and field mice, by weddings and the necks
of roosters Grandma wrung to welcome us back home
— and all the while we're talking loaves of Polish
rye are going down with butter, beer, and links
of steaming kielbasa! And everyone weeps
unable to keep his hands off the horseradish.
Then Uncle John, whose knees are pocked
with shrapnel, makes up his mind on the spot
to polka with Uncle Andy, the stiff one
who wears gartered socks. And gathered around
like this, someone always recalls a relation
burdened with more than his share of grief,
and the latest passing, the latest operation.
But always there is food on the table
and always another wedding in sight—
a beautiful cousin with red hair—
and Uncle Joe will pick up Grandma and
look! already Grandma has her glass of beer,
blushing as the young blond Polish priest
bites into his chicken next to her.

— *Gary Gildner*

: :

A Kitchen Memory

My mother is peeling an apple over the sink,
her two deft hands effortless and intent.
The skin comes away in the shape of a corkscrew,
red and white by turns, with a shimmer of rose
where the blade in its turn cuts close: a blush,
called out of hiding like a second skin.
Now the apple fattens in her hand;
the last scrap of parings falls away;
and she halves and sections the white grainy meat,
picks up another apple, brushes back
the dark hair at her temple with the knife hand.
The only sound is the fan stirring the heat.

— *Roy Scheele*

Kitchen Song

Trust a woman
to conjure joy out of pain,
out of that room I thought I'd never
want to see again. That citadel
my Mother banned me from —
sacred as her bedroom
(that private estate
of drawn shades
and headache).

My Mother's kitchen. Where my hands
betrayed me: too big,   too slow,
dirtying too many pots,
forgetting if I'd put in a pinch
or not. Her parings
were all of a piece, whole-cloth,
a magician's trick
I couldn't be taught.   My knife
seemed eternally aimed
straight for wrist or heart.
You'll be no man's wife.   Get out.

My kitchen.   Pots of dirt
for herbs: rosemary, thyme
and flowers.   Hand-potted dishes
lined up for the kittens
(yes, Mama, they have their own);
the coffee's on
and there's a man who'll eat
my success or my failure. Come,
Mama, into my kitchen —
Here's a slice
of sun and a song.

— Jeannine Dobbs

Stark County Holidays

Our mother's kingdom does not fall,
But like her old piano wanders
Slowly and finally out of tune.
There are so many things to do
She rarely plays it anymore,
But there were years of Bach and Strauss;

The chords flew black and rich and round
With meaning through our windy house.
We fell asleep, we wove our dreams
In that good wilderness of sound.

At Christmas, when we all come home,
The table's stretched with boards and laid
With linen; in a festive ring
We sit like heroes trading tales.
But lately in a little while,
Among the talk of art, or war,
A kind of hesitation comes;
A silence echoes everything.

Afterward we rise and file
Behind our mother to the fire.
With stiffened hands she thumps away
In honor of the holy day;
Hymns and carols rise and hold
As best as they can on blasted scales.
We listen, staring at the night
Where faith and failure sound their drums,
And snow is drifting mile on mile.

Our mother's kingdom does not fall,
But year by year the promise fades;
Dreams of our childhood warp and pall,
Caught in the dark fit of the world.
Now, less than what we meant to be,
We watch the night and feed the fire.
We listen as the bent chords climb
Toward alleluias rich but wrong;
We sing, and grieve for what we are
Compared with the intended song.

—Mary Oliver

Baking Day

Thursday was baking day in our house.
The spicy smell of new baked bread would meet
My nostrils when I came home from school and there would be
Fresh buns for tea, but better still were the holidays.

Then I could stay and watch the baking of the bread.
My mother would build up the fire and pull out the damper
Until the flames were flaring under the oven; while it was
   heating
She would get out her earthenware bowl and baking board.

Into the crater of flour in the bowl she would pour sugar
And yeast in hot water; to make sure the yeast was fresh
I had often been sent to fetch it from the grocer that morning,
And it smelt of the earth after rain as it dissolved in the
   sweet water.

Then her small stubby hands would knead and pummel
The dough until they became two clowns in baggy pantaloons,
And the right one, whose three fingers and blue stump
Told of the accident which followed my birth, became whole.

As the hands worked a creamy elastic ball
Took shape and covered by a white cloth was set
On a wooden chair by the fire slowly to rise:
To me the most mysterious rite of all.

From time to time I would peep at the living dough
To make sure it was not creeping out of the bowl.
Sometimes I imagined it possessed, filling the whole room,
And we helpless, unable to control its power to grow,

But as it heaved above the rim of the bowl mother
Was there, taking it and moulding it into plaited loaves
And buns and giving me a bit to make into a bread man,
With currant eyes, and I, too, was a baker.

My man was baked with the loaves and I would eat him
    for tea.
On Friday night, when the plaited loaves were placed
Under a white napkin on the dining table,
Beside two lighted candles, they became holy.

No bread will ever be so full of the sun as the pieces
We were given to eat after prayers and the cutting of this bread.
My mother, who thought her life had been narrow, did not want
Her daughters to be bakers of bread. I think she was wise.

Yet sometimes, when my cultivated brain chafes at kitchen
Tasks, I remember her, patiently kneading dough
And rolling pastry, her untutored intelligence
All bent towards nourishing her children.

— *Rosemary Joseph*

Canning Time

The floor was muddy with the juice of peaches
and my mother's thumb, bandaged for the slicing,
watersobbed. She and Aunt Wessie skinned
bushels that day, fat Georgia Belles
slit streaming into the pot. Their knives
paid out limp bands onto the heap
of parings. It took care to pack the jars,
reaching in to stack the halves

firm without bruising, and lowering
the heavy racks into the boiler already
trembling with steam, the stove malignant
in heat. As Wessie wiped her face
the kitchen sweated its sweet filth.
In that hell they sealed the quickly browning
flesh in capsules of honey, making crystals
of separate air across the vacuums.
The heat and pressure were enough to grow
diamonds as they measured hot
syrup into quarts. By supper the last jar
was set on the counter to cool
into isolation. Later in the night
each little urn would pop as it
achieved its private atmosphere and
we cooled into sleep, the stove now
neutral. The stones already
pecked clean in the yard were free to try
again for the sun. The orchard meat fixed in
cells would be taken down cellar in the
morning to stay gold like specimens
set out and labelled, a vegetal
battery we'd hook up later. The women
too tired to rest easily think of
the treasure they've laid up today
for preservation at coffin level, down there
where moth and rust and worms corrupt,
a first foundation of shells to be
fired at the winter's muddy back.

—*Robert Morgan*

··

The Gone Years

Night pockets the house
in a blue
muffle the color
of my father's Great Depression.
I see him move
over the snow, leaving
the snow unmoved.
The snow has no imagination.

My mother and I shuffle by
each other as if we were
the dead, speechless
breathers at windows done in black
oilcloth tacked down by stars.

"It's fair that his clothes be worn
out as he was." She irons them
for distant cousins, the tattersalls
sending up a hush
beneath her hands.

Through January's flannel
nights she turns old
stories over and over,
letting the gone
years hug her
with his long wool arms.

—*Alice Fulton*

The View from Father's Porch

Five hundred guests upon a summer's day,
And yet there were no roads to Kineo.
Father could step outside his store and see
The mountain like a shaggy beast that lay
Watching for steamers on the lake below.
A fleet conveyed the aristocracy
To the resort, to golf and luxury,
An island where a queen might love to go.

This afternoon my father would have wept:
The hotel toppled in the Crash, and so
The lawns, uncut, are bristling like hay;
The porch has rotted round the store he kept;
On Moosehead Lake I saw no boats except
The rented one that carried me away.

— *Celeste Turner Wright*

Among His Effects
We Found a Photograph

My mother is beautiful as a flapper.
She is so in love
that she has been gazing
secretly at my father
for forty years.
He's in uniform,
with puttees and swagger stick,
a tiny cork mustache
bobbing above a shore line of teeth.

They are "poor but happy."
In his hand is a lost book
he had memorized,
with a thousand clear answers
to everything.

— Ed Ochester

∴

Songs My Mother Taught Me

In a small throaty soprano
In perfect pitch always,
She sang "Thou Art Repose"
Before my feet could touch
The floor from the music bench
And "The Trout" — Schubert at peace
With his mildest remembrance,
Then glittering with fear.
I remember listening, awed
That her fingers touching the keys
(Too small to reach octaves)

Could clear a way for her voice
To stream through such music
Composed by real composers
Who had used just pen and ink
(A skill I'd halfway mastered
By scrawling words, not notes),
All dead, all living again
Each time she played and sang
"On Wings of Song," "Pale Hands
I Loved," *"Ich liebe dich,"*
"None But the Lonely Heart."

Now like Franz and Felix,
Amy, Edvard, and Piotr,
She depends on someone else
To sing what she dreamed of.

She has gone to her long rest
By the restless, restful waters
Of whatever Shalimar
Or Ganges she longed for
In Zeit und Ewigkeit,
Her heart no longer lonely,
And I sing this for her.

— *David Wagoner*

Music

— for my mother

When you wanted a piano
everyone wanted something:
Betty prayed for a red silk dress
with polka-dots,
Mother wanted a gold watch
to hold the time
that kept leaving her
before she could find it.
Even your father,
who spent hours calculating
figures in a checkbook,
wanted a green Studebaker car
with fat headlights,
a Venetian blind
that didn't stick.

That was the first lesson.

You made a paper keyboard
and played it in the dark,
singing the notes.
If you pressed your foot
you could feel a pedal in the carpet,
hear the murmur lasting beyond itself
the way it did when they played
the piano at school.
Everyone would turn, pack their books,
while you stood hinged to that last tone
emptying into the air. It was gone.
But if you tilted your head?

Your father found the keyboard
and slapped you for wasting paper.

The second lesson was long.

—*Naomi Shihab Nye*

Thanksgiving

The tides in my eyes are heavy.
My grandmother's house wears oakleaves
instead of nasturtiums; hollyhocks
dry in the front-porch gutter.
I must have been a bad boy,
exiled under the attic stairs:
a hardwood hatrack plants
its Black-Eyed petals under my nose,
but I have no hat to top it.
I reach, instead, to touch the face
of my mother's grandfather's clock.

My fingers tick, but the clock
will not relent; I cannot wind
nor strike it.
            I only smell
the locked closets, the open shelves
of jarred preserves that grow
their quiet mold in the old back pantry.
My ears are mice, peaked to the sizzle
of badly bottled homemade rootbeer.
It was once Thanksgiving all week.
And we ate all day from the five pies
backed in the coalstove oven — after
the peas put up from summer, and squash
put down in the cellar. I cannot say
what else lies under my tongue.
My mother's mouth is grave with snow;
on the hill where she, too, was once young.

— Philip Booth

Stonecarver

—for Father

Don't look at his hands now.
Stiff and swollen, small finger
curled in like a hermit:
needing someone to open the ketchup,
an hour to shave.
That hand held the mallet,
made the marble say
Cicero, Juno, and *laurel.*

Don't think of his eyes
behind thick lenses squinting
at headlines, his breath
drowning in stonedust and Camels,
his sparrow legs.

Think of the one who slid
3 floors down scaffolding ropes
every lunchtime,
who stood up to Donnelly the foreman
for more time to take care.

Keep him   the man in the photo,
straight-backed on the park bench
in Washington, holding hands
with your mother.
Keep his hands holding
calipers, patterns, and pointer,
bringing the mallet down
fair on the chisel,
your father's hands sweeping off dust.

— *Carole Oles*

Edwin A. Nelms

the quick flick of a smile
is still there

the curly hair still
coal black
at 67

the luminous brown
eyes softer now
mellowed
by the Valium

and the body
like a wool sweater
washed in hot water
shrunk
from six foot two
down to five foot four

bones
poke out
under his skin

his shriveled bottom
hangs in his slacks
like a limp
bean bag

brittle bone
cancer
has turned him
into a crisp cicada skin
ready to crunch
if I hug him

—*Sheryl L. Nelms*

Poem to Help My Father

When I was young, and the day
a smudged gray sketch
of house and rain and picket fence
and I knew by heart
the knotty-pine face of each room,
and my brother was being Batman
my dolls didn't feel like playing
the dog was dreaming
we were still six years from supper
and there was nothing on earth to do,
my mother would call from the kitchen,
"go bang your head against the wall."
My father, seeing my great talent
from his big leather armchair,
would say, "go write a poem."

I am older now, in a far worse afternoon.
There is cancer in my father.
Can you believe it?
Not Red Jello, not Strawberry Cheesecake,
but cancer (I won't give it a capital c, I just won't)
and the rooms have white faces, only white,
the doctor's one frail word is "treatable"
my father's leather armchair hurts him
(some friend, eh?)
and there is nothing to be done,
despite my great talent,
but bang my head against the wall
and write this poem

— *Norma Richman*

My Father's Heart

He longs to open his arms, we can see that
on his face, and boasts of being able to crack
a walnut with his fist, clenched for good measure,
a mouse in service of an elephant. The nurse
tries to improve matters, uses a hyphen-like
device, commanding the first word to follow
the second wherever it goes, up the left,
down the right. Ventricle? Auricle? All that
blood retreating to chambers and vessels
so long they could float all the king's horses.

Giddy-up, he cried when he came home, swept me
up on the arm of the couch, popped his fedora
on my head, patted my rear, giddy-up Silver!
That's what we call Waltzing Matilda down home,
the neighbor from Australia said when he came
to pay his last respects. Dad was dancing
his last, the giant was jealous, fancied
this little father of mine an object
of universal desire.

—*Stuart Friebert*

Goodbye

1

My mother, poor woman, lies tonight
in her last bed. It's snowing, for her, in her darkness.
I swallow down the goodbyes I won't get to use,
tasteless, with wretched mouth-water;
whatever we are, she and I, we're nearly cured.

The night years ago when I walked away
from that final class of junior high school students
in Pittsburgh, the youngest of them ran
after me down the dark street. "Goodbye!" she called,
snow swirling across her face, tears falling.

2

Tears have kept on falling. History
has taught them its slanted understanding
of the human face. At each last embrace the dying give,
the snow brings down its disintegrating curtain.
The mind shreds the present, once the past is over.

In the Derry graveyard where only her longings sleep
and armfuls of flowers go out in the drizzle
the bodies not yet risen must lie nearly forever . . .
"Sprouting good Irish grass," the graveskeeper blarneys,
he can't help it, "a sprig of shamrock, if they were young."

3

In Pittsburgh tonight, those who were young
will be less young, those who were old, more old, or more likely
no more; and the street where Syllest,
fleetest of my darlings, caught up with me
and hugged me and said goodbye, will be empty. Well,

one day the streets all over the world will be empty —
already in heaven, listen, the golden cobblestones have fallen still —
everyone's arms will be empty, everyone's mouth, the Derry earth.
It is written in our hearts, the emptiness is all.
That is how we have learned, the embrace is all.

— *Galway Kinnell*

∴

Father

—Theodore Briggs Kooser,
  May 19, 1902-December 31, 1979

You spent fifty-five years
walking the hard floors
of the retail business,
first, as a boy playing store

in your grandmother's barn,
sewing feathers on hats
that the neighbors threw out,
then stepping out onto

the smooth pine planks
of your uncle's grocery—
Salada Tea in gold leaf
over the door, your uncle

and father still young then
in handlebar moustaches,
white aprons with dusters
tucked into their sashes—

then to the varnished oak
of a dry goods store—
music to your ears,
that bumpety-bump

of bolts of bright cloth
on the counter tops,
the small rattle of buttons,
the bell in the register—

then on to the cold tile
of a bigger store, and then one
still bigger — gray carpet,
wide aisles, a new town

to get used to — then into
retirement, a few sales
in your own garage,
the concrete under your feet.

You had good legs, Dad,
and a good storekeeper's eye:
asked once if you remembered
a teacher of mine,

you said, "I certainly do;
size ten, a little something
in blue." How you loved
what you'd done with your life!

Now you're gone, and the clerks
are lazy, the glass cases
smudged, the sale sweaters
pulled off on the floor.

But what good times we had
before it was over:
after those stores had closed,
you posing as customers,

strutting in big flowered hats,
those aisles like a stage,
the pale mannequins watching;
we laughed till we cried.

— *Ted Kooser*

At Night

In the dust are my father's beautiful hands,
In the dust are my mother's eyes.
Here by the shore of the ocean standing,
Watching: still I do not understand.

Love flows over me, around me,
Here at night by the sea, by the sovereign sea.

Gone is that bone-hoard of strength;
Gone her gentle motion laughing, walking.

Is it not strange that disease and death
Should rest, by the undulant sea?

And I stare, rich with gifts, alone,

Feeling from the sea those terrene presences,
My father's hands, my mother's eyes.

— *Richard Eberhart*

Fall Journey

Evening came, a paw, to the gray hut by the river.
Pushing the door with a stick, I opened it.
Only a long walk had brought me there,
steps into the continent they had placed before me.

I read weathered log, stone fireplace, broken chair,
the dead grass outside under the cottonwood tree —
and it all stared back. We've met before, my memory
started to say, somewhere . . .

And then I stopped: my father's eyes were gray.

— William Stafford

My Mother's Death

It's still inside me

like that ninety-pound fibroid tumor
in that woman's womb.

Unable to lie down or walk,
she could   only kneel.

It took two doctors to lift it out of her,
the paper said.

But who will help me.

—Judith Hemschemeyer

Poem for My Father's Ghost

Now is my father
A traveler, like all the bold men
He talked of, endlessly
And with boundless admiration,

Over the supper table,
Or gazing up from his white pillow—
Book on his lap always, until
Even that grew too heavy to hold.

Now is my father free of all binding fevers.
Now is my father
Traveling where there is no road.

Finally, he could not lift a hand
To cover his eyes.
Now he climbs to the eye of the river,
He strides through the Dakotas,
He disappears into the mountains. And though he looks
Cold and hungry as any man
At the end of a questing season,

He is one of *them* now:
He cannot be stopped.

Now is my father
Walking the wind,
Sniffing the deep Pacific
That begins at the end of the world.

Vanished from us utterly,
Now is my father circling the deepest forest—
Then turning in to the last red campfire burning
In the final hills,

Where chieftains, warriors and heroes
Rise and make him welcome,
Recognizing, under the shambles of his body,
A brother who has walked his thousand miles.

—*Mary Oliver*

My Father's Ghost

—If you count nine stars and nine stones, then look into an empty room, you'll see a ghost.

—Midwestern folk belief

I counted them, and now I look through the door
Into the empty room where he was, where nine stars
Have failed to conjure him under a ceiling
Presiding over nothing except a floor
And four walls without windows, where nine stones
Have failed to call him up from the netherworld
To tell me of his cruel unnatural murder.

He stays as invisible as other souls
In either world. I have to imagine him
In this interior without natural light,
Recall him burned by splashing steel each shift
Of his unnatural life, his thigh broken
To an Oedipal limp, his eyes half-blinded
By staring into the pits of open hearths,
His memory put to sleep, his ears deafened
By the slamming of drop-forges and the roar
Of fire as bright as the terrible hearts of stars,
Of fire that would melt stones. He won't come back
At anyone's bidding in his hard-hat of a helmet,
His goggles up like a visor, but I dream him
Returning unarmed, unharmed. Words, words. I hold
My father's ghost in my arms in his dark doorway.

— David Wagoner

Remembering My Father

As I seize the ladder by its shoulder
blades and shake it back and forth
to test its roots, its cling, test
with gummed toes each rung up
from the shadow of the north wall
into the bright desert of the roof
the sun's weight spreads over my back,
and I see my father frowning in the sun,
his freckled back zigzagged with peeling
tan, his shoulders red, lowering a rock
into the stone swimming pool he built
by hand with boulders slithered
down on sledges from the woods,
split, rinsed off and fit — a pool
I could dive into until my ears
were so waterclogged they croaked.
I reach the top, fit
the window frame in place — the corners
mate — aim the first nail away
from the glass, sink it to its chin,
finger the next nail and prick
the wood; but as I heft the framing
hammer back to stroke, I see my father
in the cellar, frowning as he fits
his saw blade to a line, eases it back
and forth to start the cut, his breath
hissing through his nose as it always does
when he's intent. I hear my own breath
hissing through my nose. Something
silent in me starts chuckling in pure
gaiety because I'm frowning too, because
I know exactly what I look like.

— Jonathan Holden

: :

Visit

Here, in my parents' home
on this cold night in February,
I turn off the reading lamp,
and look out of what used to be
my bedroom window.
A rabbit kicks up snow, leaving
its tracks across Lynch's side yard.
On the distant hills, where the sky darkens,
I count seven towers.
As before, I know they are there
by the rows of red blinking stars.

I have not come back here
to look out of the window at snow
lining the woods between black trees,
and to listen to cars shifting gears
on the road beside Camp Horne Creek
where I caught salamanders,
and brought them home for pets,
thinking love could make them live
longer than two weeks.
Could some of the people in those cars
be traveling to their parents' homes
in the same way I have traveled,
hoping to ask my mother and father
for forgiveness for the years
they have taken from their lives?

— *Vic Coccimiglio*

Strings:
From Brothers and Sisters

Brother

you still carry
your guilt around for company
I will not deprive you of it
but I have an empty space
where my hate lived
while I nursed it
as if it were a child

brother my only
brother it was too late for us
before we were born

it was too late
before you learned to be brutal
and I learned to be weak

your childhood was a hallway of doors
each closing just as you
got to it
but I was younger
and all the doors were closed
before I could walk
how could I have expected you
to save me when you could
not save yourself

brother my only
brother if not from you
from whom did I learn
so much despair

I went in search
of a father and found you
with a whip in your hand
but what were you searching for
in such dark places
where I was searching for love

— Richard Shelton

Lantern

Hours late and afraid to go in,
You lay on a couch of raked leaves,
Your thumb stuck in a bottle
Because Father was a blue shadow
In front of TV and Uncle traced
And retraced his tattoos in private.
It was cold in there, hands like a scuttle
Of leaves under exhaust fumes.

You climbed the peach tree and stared over
At the junkyard, at a dog circling
Among the scaffolds of old plumbing.
Far away, a warm length of neon and warehouses
Slamming shut, goggled workers shivering
In broken light. Father called. You turned
And he was below, shirtless, a rolled newspaper . . .
He called again, then went inside
That darkened window by window.

When Uncle shouted promises
You jumped down and didn't know
It was over — the joy of sparrows,
Of rocks you had crayoned faces on,
Of kites falling noiselessly as smoke.

In that quiet you could hear the house
Tick under their footsteps. You raised
the bottle like a lantern at the front window,
And suddenly saw them for the first time
By the same light that gave you away.

— *Gary Soto*

In the Motel

Bouncing! bouncing! on the beds
My brother Bob and I cracked heads —

People next door heard the crack,
Whammed on the wall, so we whammed right back.

Dad's razor caused an overload
And wow! did the TV set explode!

Someone's car backed fast and — tinkle!
In our windshield was a wrinkle.

Eight more days on the road? Hooray!
What a bang-up holiday!

— *X. J. Kennedy*

The Dirty-Billed Freeze Footy

Remember that Saturday morning
Mother forgot the word gull?

We were all awake but still in bed
and she called out, "Hey kids!

What's the name of that bird that eats garbage
and stands around in cold water on the beach?"

And you, the quick one, the youngest daughter
piped right back: "A dirty-billed freeze footy!"

And she laughed till she was weak,
until it hurt her.   And you had done it:

reduced our queen to warm and helpless rubble.

And the rest of the day, baking or cleaning
or washing our hair until it squeaked,

whenever she caught sight of you
it would start all over again.

—*Judith Hemschemeyer*

To My Blood Sister

—for Rosemary

Yes, I was the head of our Halloween horse—
And you, and you, the rump,
Swaggering behind,
Blind to our mad journey into the night.

Yes, it was I who grabbed the best dolls.
It was I who demanded the better bed, jumping with
Victory on those firm springs.
And I dominated
The bathtub—
Water splashing with
Whip-dip games and soapy speeches.

I was first to birthday parties, horseshows,
Bike trips, school dances, bracelets from boyfriends, and
Luscious halter-dress evening gowns.
Yes, and it was I who painted, played my flute, and
Cantered over you and your humble Raggedy Ellen
Like a hurricane of colts.
My feet firm in the stirrups,
I held tight to the reins—
Up front,
Wings to the wind.

But now, dear sister,
It is you who rescues me
From the creases—
Those places below the surface I could not see
When I galloped so fast.

You knew them, though—
Those troughs of fear.
You, whose lips were once puffed and
Pale with panic;
Afraid to go to school, afraid you'd faint
In your desk in Miss Kerner's class;
Your fingers used to swell
In church. You even feared
The pillow at night—
Paralyzed by the terror of suffocating,
Letting go, and falling backwards.
Now I know.

And it is you, strong sister
Who offers me a handkerchief
Filled with sweet smells and normality.
Your lips are now rosy with confidence —
You are more beautiful than you have ever been.

I love you
My sane and shapely sister
With the thick black hair and jettisons of laughter.
You run deeper than I ever imagined.
Take the reins for me, will you?

— Christine E. Hemp

Icicle

I smacked you in the mouth for no good reason
except that the icicle had broken off
so easily and that it felt like a club
in my hand, and so I swung it, the soft
pad of your lower lip sprouting a drop,
then gushing a trail onto the snow even
though we both squeezed the place with our fingers.
I'd give a lot not to be the swinger
of that icicle. I'd like another
morning just like that, cold, windy, and bright
as Russia, your glasses fogging up, your face
turning to me again. I tell you I might
help both our lives by changing that act to this,
by handing you the ice, a gift, my brother.

— David Huddle

The Little Brother Poem

I keep seeing your car in the streets
but it never turns at our corner. I keep finding
little pieces of junk you saved, a packing box, a white rag,
and stashed in the shed for future uses. Today I am cleaning
the house. I take your old camping jug, poke my finger
through the rusted hole in the bottom, stack it on the trash
wondering if you'd yell at me, if you had other plans for it.

Little brother, when you were born I was glad. Believe this.
There is much you never forgave me for but I tell you now,
I wanted you.

It's true there are things I would change. Your face bleeding
the day you followed me and I pushed you in front of a bicycle.
For weeks your eyes hard on me under the bandages. For years
you quoted me back to myself, mean things I'd said that I didn't
remember. Last summer you disappeared into the streets of Dallas
at midnight on foot crying and I realized you'd been serious,
some strange bruise you still carried under the skin.

Little brother, it's easy to write you a poem.
I've never done it before but today it's easier than talking
or walking around feeling sad about the fact you're not here.

You're not little anymore. You passed me up and kept reminding
me I'd stopped growing. We're different, always have been,
you're Wall Street and I'm the local fruit market,
you're Pierre Cardin and I'm a used bandanna.
That's fine, I'll take differences over things that match.

If you were here today we wouldn't say all this.
You'd be outside cranking up the lawnmower.
I'd be in here answering mail.
You'd pass through the house and say "You're a big help"
and I'd say "Don't mention it" and the door would close.

I think of the rest of our lives. You're on the edge of yours today.
Long-distance I said "Are you happy?" and your voice wasn't sure.
It sounded small, younger, it sounded like the little brother
I don't have anymore, the one who ran miniature trucks up my
arms telling me I was a highway, the one who believed me
when I told him monkeys arrived in the night to kidnap boys
with brown hair. I'm sorry for everything I did that hurt.
It's a large order I know, dumping out a whole drawer at once,
fingering receipts and stubs, trying to put them back
in some kind of shape so you'll be able to find everything later,
when you need it, and you don't have so much time.

— *Naomi Shihab Nye*

Family Cups

I place two cups beside each other
And all the confused voices return
Bickering for a place at the table.
These two cups are fragile
As the moments before a family dinner
When the mother is too busy
To polish the silverware
And the father is attentive
To the two boys made of metal
As they play with toys and make a clamor.

Two cups on a table, wide-open flowers
Eager for a common life. But
Something is lacking, someone
Is too happy, someone is angry,
Stirring the grounds in a jealous cup.

Coffee you can't see through
Is a humble substance. Over the steam
And the image of a face, we sit down
Or stand up, excusing ourselves.
A family at dinner is one long drama,
Needing that frame to be heroic.
These two cups, chipped cold pleasures
Of the mouth, fill, are emptied, filled,
That after dinner two boys may stare
Out a window at stars lighting up,
Filling the heavens' faces, where
Each of them wanders in his solitude.
The first sorrow comes from the first hope.

— *Steve Orlen*

At the Grave of My Brother

The mirror cared less and less at the last, but
the tone of his voice roamed, had more to find,
back to the year he was born; and the world
that saw him awhile again went blind.

Drawn backward along the street, he disappeared
by the cedars that faded a long time ago
near the grave where Mother's hair was a screen
but she was crying. I see a sparrow

Chubby like him, full of promise, barely
holding a branch and ready to fly.
In his house today his children begin
to recede from this year and go their own way.

Brother: Good-bye.

— *William Stafford*

Strings:
From Cousins

Cousin Ella Goes to Town

Now you have to promise
you won't breathe a word of this.
It was after Brian died.
You know I got me a little insurance money
and I said to myself, Eller,
what kind of life have you had
and what are you likely to get
and you know the answer to that.
Not much.

Seemed like all I'd ever done
was dump pennies from a jar.
Brian left me just enough
to stay on in this house
sewing and tending other people's kids
fading out like an old TV.
So I took a hard look.
And do you know what I did?

I went to Louisville.
Yessir, I got on the Greyhound bus
rode right there
and took a taxi to the Galt House.
And for four days
I had me a room
and I pretended
to be somebody else.

Lord, children, I ate the best food
went to dress stores and picture shows
I even called my name different.
And do you know
I got so high and mighty
with my new hairdo—

I had the yellow scared out of this wad
got me a city style —
that on the third night
right before the Icecapades
I was trying on this hat
and I saw my face all gaudy in that mirror
and my freckled hands with peach polish on each nail
and I took to crying
for all the world like Brian had died again.

I grabbed a washrag
and scrubbed my face.
I snatched them bobby pins out of my hair
and brushed it till my scalp
stung like fire.
And honey I got out of there.

By the time the bus let me off
I was plumb out of tears.
I just marched in
put my pocketbook down —
I'd left everything but a raincoat
at the hotel —
I rolled down my stockings
heated up some soup
sat in my chair
and read the Sunday School lesson.
Next morning I tried
to wear that coat to church
but you know it never fit me right
at all.

— *George Ella Lyon*

Man and Machine

Besides drinking and telling lies,
nothing interested my cousin Luther
like working with the tractor.
Astride that bright and smelly beast
he was a man inspired.
Revving and tearing the stubble
of early spring he cussed
the metal like a favorite mule,
parrying with the shift any stallout.
In too big a hurry to turn
at the end of a row he jammed
in a brake and spun around,
lowered the harrows
into the winter-bleached field
and blasted off for yon end.
Barely able to read he took
dusters and bush hogs and diesel movements
apart with the skill of a surgeon,
hollering on the phone for parts
as far away as Charlotte or Atlanta.
Would stay on his ass at the filling station
or country store for weeks
while wife and kids and parents
picked in the heat the crops he'd
drive to market. Neither storm-threat
nor overripening could move him
to join their labor. Until time
for dusting with the homemade blower
mounted on a jeep. Or after the vines
were cut he'd windlass in the long wires.
Winters Luther lived only for his truck,
banging down the dirt road to Chestnut Springs
for booze and women. But that was just

occasional. Most days he'd brag at the store
about his pickup, or be trading for another
with even thicker tires, more horsepower
and chrome, a gunrack in the window.
At home he'd maybe tune a little,
oil the plates of the planter.
But off the machine he was just
another stocky hoojer, yelling
to make up for his lack of size
and self-esteem, adding fat and blood
pressure. Late February breaking time
transformed him. He leapt on the big
diesel and burned out its winter farts
all the way to the bottoms, whipping
the animal until it glowed, became
his legs and voice and shoulders.
To children and himself he tore up ground
like a centaur. Plowing with the lights on
all night in the river fields
he circled more times than any race driver.
shouting in the settling damp while
we slept hearing the distant fury.
And by morning the fields were new.

— *Robert Morgan*

Slow Waker

I look at the cousin,
eighteen, across the breakfast.
He had to be called and called.
He smiles, but without
conviction. He will not

have tea, oh OK,
if it's no trouble,
he will have tea.

His adult face is brand-new.
Once the newness
clears up and it has got
an expression or two
besides bewilderment
he could be a handsome
devil. He could be
a carpenter, a poet, it's
all possible . . .
impossible. The future
is not a word in his mouth.

That, for him, is the trouble:
he lay in bed caught deep
in the mire between
sleep and awake, neither
alert nor resting,
between the flow of night,
ceaselessly braiding itself,
and the gravelly beach
that our soles have thickened on.

Nobody has ever told him
he is goodlooking,
just that his feet smell.

He paces through alien London
all day. Everything
is important and unimportant.
He feeds only by osmosis.
He stares at the glint
and blunt thrust of traffic. He
wants to withdraw.

He wants to withdraw into
a small space, like
the cupboard under the stairs
where the vacuum cleaner is kept,
so he can wait, and doze,
and get in nobody's way.

— Thom Gunn

Helen's Scar

Helen, my cousin, says she still has the scar
from the time I pushed her out of the plum tree.

I don't even remember the plum tree.

"It must have been an accident," I say to her.
"It was no accident," she says. "You were mad at me."
She laughs. "It bled like the devil. I was scared to death."

How old were we then? Ten or eleven,
which means that she's seen that scar every day
for close to forty years
and will continue to see it
for the rest of her life.
It's not bad. But it's always there.

I did it;
and I don't even remember the plum tree.

—Alden Nowlan

Strings:
From Nieces and Nephews

Croquet

This decorous, nineteenth-century
entertainment my Newbern grandmother
and great aunts come down from front porch rocking chairs
to play an afternoon hot enough to smother
Methodist ladies who say their prayers
at night but who croquet in quiet fury:
Gran gathers her concentration, pauses,
then lets her red mallet fly forth, causes
her skirt to follow her follow-through, then sweeps
it down and follows her red ball. Two wicked
split-shots Aunt Iva fires. Aunt Stella, whom
polio crippled in childhood, makes wicket
after wicket, strikes the post, and in diningroom
tones says, "Keep your manners but play for keeps."

— David Huddle

Aunt Melissa

had perfect pitch
but was not a Christian woman
like her Baptist sister.
Had nipples I saw
through a knot hole
black as a birddog's lip.
Moved across the room
in ways that made looking
a sin. I loved
to watch the sweat
run down her neck and
disappear. Her flesh
was a dulcimer's hourglass

feathered to music
each time she spoke.
Some dark notes
a teenboy learns from kin,
I heard her sing
in songs not hymns,
burning my bones to a blindness
of youth that helps me
see the beauty of the air,
saves me from unearned
mysteries.

— *R. T. Smith*

Mac

"Good Egg" — her favorite words
for those she liked — beyond that,
all was Irish flare and curse.
She had a temper made for feuds
and kept her whiskey in the fridge
so she wouldn't have to fool with ice.
And when they cut her open just to find
they couldn't stop the cancer,
she went back to the nursing home
from which she'd just retired
as head nurse —
helpless, hairless, strangely mute.
And if they ever stopped to watch
the terrible irony at work
they never seemed to show it —
condescending, starched, and vague.
Old women die of cancer every day,
even the tough and lonely ones
stripped of all but the crying out.

Was she patient here or nurse?

She used to tell stories of the ones
whose age had finally snapped —
night walkers, shriekers, babblers,
old men running naked in the halls.
I never heard her speak
of those who only had to wait,
nor the hands that must have reached out.
But then, this page is cold
with all that I've forgotten,
my last and only Irish aunt:
Good night, Old Dear, "Good Egg."

—*Mark Vinz*

Uncle Claude

Uncle Claude on the davenport,
drowsy with heartburn, was
the horizon wearing a tee-shirt.

But that was the night, after
supper, his chest got anchor
heavy. Heavier. All he could do was
keep his eyes open and breathe
slow, and feel it happen: himself and
the davenport crashing through the
frontroom floor, then the basement —
demolishing the clotheslines —
on through a slab of concrete
foundation, then miles and miles
of black dirt and rock and out
into the sparkling stars, and

all the way he couldn't help
cussing out his job, his wife,
the house and yard, the gas
company, lawnmower, car, even that
tiny davenport-shaped pinhole of
light in the frontroom floor,
too far away to matter now,
before he hit bottom.

—*David Allan Evans*

The Musician at His Work

Again the belt was off the flywheel
A fraction of an inch too loose
Eddie Yarrow guessed
One of these days he'd get it fixed
maybe when the summer fallow's done
He jumped into a rigid trough of earth
grabbed the belt as he had done
so many times before
slipped the belt around the spinning wheel
which spun his hand around
lopped his fingers off
dropped them like stones
four stones white and still
on the unturned earth
He watched his hand
turn to blood
felt the pain
greater than pain
knew exactly
what it meant

—*Robert Currie*

Forget About It

Uncle Eddie told him how it was
  Lots of times Yarrow it's   well
  just like my fingers was still there
  On a chilly day   why
  I can feel a kind of tingling
  underneath the nails
  like the tips going numb
  All I have to do
  is close my eyes
  and I can move my fingers
  Hell sometimes I'd even swear
  they're picking out a tune.

His uncle saw the look on Yarrow's face
  Ah it ain't so bad this way
  Might've been a power take-off
  like Walt Thurgood south of town
  caught his overalls in one
  and nobody missed him till dark
  Coming across the south 40
  they heard the engine and a slapping sound
  Who knows how many hundred times
  That power take-off had
  hammered him against the ground?
  When they got the engine stopped
  nobody wanted to hold the flashlight on him

Uncle Eddie paused a moment
  No it ain't so bad this way
  Might even make things easier
  Being rid of possibilities
  maybe I'll forget what could've been

— *Robert Currie*

What He Saw

Yarrow hears the scream
runs toward the barn
but halfway there
his mother stops him
pushes him away
Her face has turned to snow
   You mustn't look she says
   mustn't look mustn't

From the darkness of his room
Yarrow sees inside the barn
Moonlight drops on Major's stall
In the shadows of the loft
harness hangs along the wall
and someone's slashing at a rope
Even when he looks away
he sees his uncle's body fall

— *Robert Currie*

Rope and Drum

That night in the barn
he saw boots in the shadows
boots turning a circle slowly
the boots on the man
who was dead

He heard drums   burial drums
hoofbeats like drumming
squeals whinnies closing around him

he lay in the stall
the bit in his mouth
cutting his flesh his screams
the stallion wild/above him
something dark   hanging
and he was hanging too

He woke with a hand on his mouth
pain in the hand
teeth in the flesh of his hand
his temples beating
the room spinning slowly
again to silence
the rope burns still
hot on his neck

— Robert Currie

Aunt Elsie's Night Music

1

Aunt Elsie hears
Singing in the night,
So I am sent running
To search under the trees.
I stand in the dark hearing nothing—
Or, at least, not what she hears—
Uncle William singing again
Irish lullabies.
I stay awhile, then turn and go inside.
Uncle William's been dead for years.

2

Climbing the steps, I think of what to say:
"I saw a bird stretching its wings in the moonlight."
"There were marks on the grass—maybe they were footprints."
"Next time I'll be quicker."

3

She's as wrinkled as a leaf
You carry in your pocket for a charm
And fold and unfold.
She's so old there's no hope.
She's so crazy there's no end
To the things she thinks are happening:
Strangers have taken her house,
They have stolen her kitchen,
They have put her in a cold bed.

4

It is summer. The singing grows urgent.
Twice a week, sometimes more,
I am called from sleep to walk in the night
And think of death.

I have been to the graveyard.
I have seen Uncle William's name
Written in stone.

I snap off the flashlight
And come in from the darkness under the trees
To the bedroom. Aunt Elsie is waiting.
I lean close to the pink ear.

5

Maybe this is what love is,
And always will be, all my life.

Whispering,
I give her an inch of hope

To bite on, like a bullet.

—*Mary Oliver*

The Great Aunts of My Childhood

Buns harden like pomanders
at their napes, their famous good
skin is smocked like cloth.
Stained glass wrings out the light
and the old tub claws the oilcloth.
Kit makes cups of bitter cocoa
or apricot juice that furs my throat.
Mame dies quietly in the bedroom.

She pressed the gold watch
into my hands, wanted me to take
her middle name at confirmation:
Zita, Saint of Pots and Pans;
but I chose Theresa, The Little Flower,
a face in the saint's book
like a nosegay. I chose this

blonde room sprouting jade
plants, electric necessities
and nights that turn
my nipples to cloves
till dawn pours in like washwater
to scrub the floors
with harsh yellow soap.

—*Alice Fulton*

The Ascension: 1925

Step on it, said Aunt Alice, *for God's sake,*
The bloody thing is going up at four!
She crammed two broilers in a paper sack,
Harnessed the dog and pushed us out the door.
Flapping like a witch, our touring car
Ate black macadam toward Fort Frontenac
Where, trembling in her ropes, the ship of air
Rolled easy as a fifty-cent cigar.

Jesus, said Uncle Lester, *what a beaut!*
Chomping on Juicy Fruit, we eyed her close
As, nuzzling upward from her stake, she rose
In strict submission to the absolute.
We hit the highway sixty on the nose
And jettisoned our chicken bones en route.

—*John Malcolm Brinnin*

Aunt Gladys's Home Movie No. 31, Albert's Funeral

Narration: Aunt Dessie, Eunice, Cora, Frankie, Gladys, Uncle Martin,
    Hubert, Charles, Bestrum.
Sound: Music from "Gunsmoke" in the TV room where the children are.

Our chairs drawn to one end of the living
room, we sit like faithful at a Sunday evening
service, viewing a miracle. Before our eyes
Albert stirs in the ticking coil of dark
film and comes riding a beam of light,
a smear of colors, finger painting — flowers.

Focus it better, Martin. It's flowers. Flowers
in Albert's garden. Not another living
soul loved flowers like Albert. Look how the light
falls over those. Must've been late in the evening.
La, la, that's pretty! What do you call that dark
red one, Glad? If that's not a sight for sore eyes!

Santa! It's Albert. The boys can't believe their eyes.
There they are, Glad. Poinsettias. Christmas flowers,
we always called them. What's that one? bloomed in the dark
in the cellar after Albert gave it up ever living.
Like four o'clocks. They don't open till the evening
shade hits em, won't open in bright light.

You took that, Glad. — Bestrum, you're in my light.
Albert caught one! Look at the boys — eyes
big as saucers! The ocean's pretty in the evening
like that. Charleston Gardens. With all those flowers
I bet Albert just thought of going and living
there. That's laurel on the parkway, it was too dark —

But if it had a bloom, it was never too dark
for Albert. He always used to make light
of his movies. I always said he could make a living
taking pictures. They say some men's eyes
got dollar signs in em. Albert had flowers
in his. He was in that garden every evening

after supper. He was in it morning *and* evening.
There it is. The boys — so grown-up in their dark
suits. That wreath — made from some of the flowers
he grew. They don't show up good here, the light
under the tent's too dim. But I never laid eyes
on prettier flowers at a funeral in all my living

days. Lights, somebody! You know those evening flowers
that open in the dark — Well, now Glad, dry your eyes,
honey. You have to close your mind and go on living!

—*Jim Wayne Miller*

At the Funeral of Great-Aunt Mary

1

Here we are, all dressed up to honor death!
No, it is not that;
It is to honor this old woman
Born in Bellingham.

2

The church windows are open to the green trees.
The minister tells us that, being
The sons and daughters of God,
We rejoice at death, for we go
To the mansions prepared
From the foundations of the world.
Impossible. No one believes it.

3

Out on the bare, pioneer field,
The frail body must wait till dusk
To be lowered
In the hot and sandy earth.

— *Robert Bly*

Strings:
From Grandchildren

Both My Grandmothers

Both my grandmas came from far away
on the difficult journey alone with their children.
They had the courage to do that
but only enough strength
to get here, raise their kids, and die.
I myself have stood on the shore of the Caspian Sea
crying my eyes out
and knowing how far away far can be
and how far this America — strange and difficult even for me —
was from their homes,
from the life they yearned back to.
But they lived here uprooted the rest of their lives.

You died, dear ones, not knowing
that your grandson loved you
and would remember you one day when he was fifty
and need you, and wish, my angels, you were there.
Eat, eat, *tottele,* you would say
if you saw me crying now.
For you were so humble
you could not believe you had anything else to offer.
And maybe eating is life's one reliable consolation
after all the disappointments
and the anguish of your children's lives.

You are long gone, my grandmas, darlings.
People are so fragile
and it is impossible to protect our dear ones
from the terrible things that happen to them,
that we do to them.
Our fate seems always to lose
our homes, our loved ones, forever.
But, my little mothers, I must tell you
that this year I went to Jerusalem, our golden city.

How you would have loved it there
in our homeland, where the heart is full.
Even if it was denied you in your lifetimes
I know that's where your spirits went when you died.
For surely that is what called me there—
they have returned to The Land, our land.

Help me, courageous ones, help me
stand up for my people, for Israel, for myself,
although frankly I feel a man is not worth anything.
Only as a Jew perhaps am I worth anything.

I know when I think of you, my grandmas,
that you are the connection with my ancestors
whom I have somehow lost.
How did the energy line get broken?
When you crossed the sea?
When I grew up an American, different from my father
but as he wanted me to be,
not speaking his heart's language or knowing the synagogue?
So I go on crying all my life,
for you, for me, for my ma,
still afraid of the dark, afraid of the man who will come get me,
and most of all afraid of the power in me
that life has not used.

I won't ever forget you again.

— Edward Field

Mardi Gras / Grandmothers
Portrait in Red and Black Crayon

As I see them now and then
one was fat and one was thin
one pushed me out   one held me in.

One created family disgraces
dyed her hair red and danced
her way to Acapulco making
clown lipstick faces.
The other wore mourning
and old creole laces

the two grandmothers I had.

::

My Irish grandmother
big Nana of the rose hats
and spaghetti-strap dresses
danced on Mardi Gras floats
until she was seventy-five
with her bonbon hair-do's
and her high-gloss Plymouth
and her hot hotel suite
with her great dripping chins
a languishing sea turtle
in the Parade of Isis.

A Real Story

Sucking on hard candy
to sweeten the taste
of old age,
grandpa told us stories
about chickens,
city chickens sold
for Sabbath soup
but rescued at the end
by some chicken-loving
providence.

Now at ninety-five,
sucked down
to nothing himself,
he says he feels
a coldness;
perhaps the coldness David felt
even with Abishag
in his bed
to warm
his chicken-thin bones.

But when we say
you'll soon get well,
grandpa pulls the sheet
over his face,
raising it between us
the way he used to raise
the Yiddish paper
when we said
enough chickens
tell us a real story.

— *Linda Pastan*

Grandfather's Heaven

My grandfather told me I had a choice.
Up or down, he said. Up or down.
He never mentioned east or west.

Grandpa stacked newspapers on his bed
and read them years after the news was relevant.
He even checked the weather reports.

Grandma was afraid of Grandpa
for some reason I never understood.
She tiptoed while he snored, rarely disagreed.

I liked Grandma because she gave me cookies
and let me listen to the ocean in her shell.
Grandma liked me even though my daddy was a Moslem.

I think Grandpa liked me too
though he wasn't sure what to do with it.
Just before he died, he wrote me a letter.

"I hear you're studying religion," he said.
"That's how people get confused.
Keep it simple. Down or up."

—*Naomi Shihab Nye*

Killing the Rooster

Gramps held the rooster
with his left hand
and swung the
ax with his right

the silver edge
sliced clean
and whumped
into the elm stump
where it stuck
handle up

the red-combed
head lay
staring
off of the stump
looking sideways across the garden

at the bronze body
flapping wings
lunatic hopping
spurting blood
and feathers
out among the rows of green onions

—*Sheryl L. Nelms*

Cleaning the Well

Each spring there was the well to be cleaned.
On a day my grandfather would say,
"It's got to be done. Let's go." This time
I dropped bat and glove, submitted to the rope,
and he lowered me into the dark and cold
water of the well. The sun
slid off at a crazy cant and I
was there, thirty feet down, waist deep
in icy water, grappling for whatever
was not pure and wet and cold.

The sky hovered like some pale moon
above, eclipsed by his heavy red face
bellowing down to me not to dally,
to feel deep and load the bucket.
My feet rasped against cold stone,
toes selecting unnatural shapes, curling
and gripping, raising them to my fingers,
then into the bucket and up to him:
a rubber ball, pine cones, leather glove,
beer can, fruit jars, an indefinable bone.
It was a time of fears: suppose he
should die or forget me, the rope break,
the water rise, a snake strike, the
bottom give way, the slick sides crumble?

The last bucket filled, my grandfather
assured, the rope loop dropped to me
and I was delivered by him who
sent me down, drawn slowly to sun
and sky and his fiercely grinning face.
"There was something else down there:
a cat or possom skeleton, but it
broke up, I couldn't pick it up."
He dropped his yellow hand on my head.
"There's always something down there
you can't quite get in your hands.
You'd know that if it wasn't your first
trip down. You'll know from now on."

"But what about the water?
Can we keep on drinking it?"

"You've drunk all that cat
you're likely to drink. Forget it
and don't tell the others. It's just
one more secret you got to live with."

— *Paul Ruffin*

My Grandfather Burning Cornfields

The only light at this hour
is the frost dusting
the flat December ground.
A shoal of thrushes
pours off the barn roof,
then banks east
into the dark of year's end.
Sleepless, I leave my bed
and go out under the sycamores
into the pull of a grief
that often comes late at night.
Across my backyard, I feel
the cold as it deepens,
moving in like a close relative.
On nights like this my grandfather lived
in his cornfields, setting the fires
meant to purify earth for new plowing.
What a privacy he enclosed there.
He kept his fires small, whispery,
their aura no brighter than
the underside of a ground dove's wing.
I recall one night watching
him, the fires underlighting his face
so that he looked like a woodcut.
I remember his breath hovering
before him like a song for which

he had no words. And my song,
which I make up tonight out of nothing,
I begin to hum as if it could
move me toward the light coming
on behind the lowest poplar trees,
the wind finally bearing away
the darkness that is
a flock of small birds.

— *Roger Sauls*

Great-Grandma

Back in a melon-pink
time she learned to write
what they call a fine hand.

At eighty she wrote the same
way, tough-nibbed and Christian
she crossed all her t's
with crescent fish, drew scallops
of galloping m's, tight
little o's and cups
of c, big W birds,
sun-slit e's.

Her signature, shirred
from end to end,
a ruffle of ink
unrolling her name,
        Respectfully
            and/or lovingly,
                Catherine

— *Carol Shields*

··

In Grandfather's Glasses

They cloud the mirror, when I put them on,
The way a leaf spatters a clear pond or
Snow pounds like breath upon a window pane.

Their velvet box was hidden
By an oil slick of scarves like
A creature crouching in bright leaves.

And when I put them on their fine gold wires wormed into
    my ears like
Tuning forks or high-pitched tones that
Dynamite minature bones shivering like flecks of dust in light.

Yet when he died I didn't mourn the way my sister
Did. I walked to school and
She was taxied past me in the car;

Tears raked her eyes like acid or a claw but
I saw her, though bleating like a black sheep with
My sympathetic gang.

But that was overshadowed as a childhood fright until
Today I saw
His glazed sight tap our mother's window like a

Cane or
Moth or
Plane clenched in insubstantial clouds tattering like cobwebs
    on wings catching flame.

— *Patricia Peters*

Yonosa House

She stroked molten tones
from the heart-carved maple dulcimer.
My grandma did.
She sat like a noble sack of bones
withered within coarse skin,
rocking to snake or corn tunes,
music of passing seasons.
She sang the old songs.

Her old woman's Tuscarora uncut hair
hung like waxed flax ready to spin
till she wove it to night braids,
and two tight-knotted ropes
lay like lanyards on her shoulders.
On my young mind she wove
the myths of the race
in fevered patterns, feathery colors:
Sound of snow, kiss of rock,
the feel of bruised birch bark,
the call of the circling hawk.

Her knotted hands showing slow blue rivers
jerked nervously through cornbread frying,
pressed fern patterns on butter pats,
brewed sassafras tea in the hearth.
She wore her lore and old age home.

They burned Yonosa in a doeskin skirt,
beads and braids, but featherless,
like a small bird with clipped wings.
I cut hearts on her coffin lid,
wind-slain maple like the dulcimer.
The mountain was holy enough for Yonosa.

We kept our promise and raised no stone.
She sank like a root to be red Georgia clay.
No Baptist churchyard caught her bones.

I thank her hands when the maple leaves turn,
hear her chants in the thrush's song.

—*R. T. Smith*

Remedies

For a cough
Inhale the ashes of a pig's snout

For color blindness
Wash your brow where a peacock has drunk

For a canker
Large or small   sip the yoke
Of a turkey egg a thimble at a time

For a sty
Wink for every crack stepped on

Let Grandma come in without knocking
Let her light the taper whose smoke
Is a braid of white grass
Let her hang
The Virgin of Guadalupe
Above your bed

The tea she has brought is to be drunk
With a thick pucker   her rosary
Placed at your hands   It won't
Be long before the pain
Napping in you
Yawns and blinks awake
And Grandma hums   prays   hums

— *Gary Soto*

White Autumn

She had always loved to read, even
in childhood during the Confederate War,
and built the habit later of staying up
by the oil lamp near the fireplace after
husband and children slept, the scrub-work done.
She fed the addiction in the hard years
of Reconstruction and even after
her husband died and she was forced
to provide and be sole foreman of the place.
While her only son fought in France
it was this second life, by the open window
in warm months when the pines on the hill
seemed to talk to the creek, or katydids
lined-out their hymns in the trees beyond the barn,
or by the familiar of fire in winter,
that sustained her. She and her daughters
later forgot the time, the exact date,
if there was such a day, she made her decision.
But after the children could cook
and garden and milk and bring in a little
by housecleaning for the rich in Flat Rock,

and the son returned from overseas
wounded but still able and married a war widow,
and when she had found just the right chair,
a rocker joined by a man over on Willow
from rubbed hickory, with cane seat and back,
and arms wide enough to rest her everlasting cup
of coffee on, or a heavy book,
she knew she had come to her place and would stay.
And from that day, if it was one time and not
a gradual recognition, she never crossed a threshold
or ventured from that special seat of rightness,
of presence and pleasure, except to be helped to bed
in the hours before dawn for a little nap.
That chair—every Christmas someone gave her a bright
cushion to break in—was the site on which she bathed
in a warm river of books and black coffee,
varieties of candy and cakes kept in a low cupboard
at hand. The cats passed through her lap and legs
and through the rungs of her seat. The tons
of firewood came in cold and left as light, smoke, ash.
She rode that upright cradle to sleep
and through many long visits with the tiers of family,
kissing the babies like different kinds of fruit.
Always hiding the clay pipe in her cabinet
when company appeared. She chaired decisions
to keep the land and refused welfare.
On that creaking throne she ruled a tiny kingdom
through war, death of kin. Even on the night she did
stop breathing, near a hundred, no one knew
exactly when, but found the lamp still on,
the romance open to a new chapter,
and the sun just appearing at her elbow.

— *Robert Morgan*

:.
:.

My Grandfather Dying

I could see bruises or shadows
deep under his skin, like the shapes
skaters find frozen in rivers —
leaves caught in flight,
or maybe the hand of a man reaching up
out of the darkness for help.

I was helpless as flowers
there at his bedside. I watched
his legs jerk in the sheets.
He answered doors,
he kicked loose stones from his fields.
I leaned down to call out my name
and he called it back. His breath
was as sour as an orchard
after the first frost.

— *Ted Kooser*

When the Ambulance Came

When the ambulance came for Grandma
that day in Easter snow
I watched them lift the stretcher
through the kitchen door.

One attendant stood in mud by
the steps where we threw the
dishwater and leftovers for the chickens:
I saw a piece of cabbage stick on

his shoe. Another wet
his glasses in the droplets
from the eave that stained the sheet as they
lowered her strapped to a tray
into the wailing oven.
Grandma had sat wrapped in the corner
for weeks protesting her
health before screaming.

Her head shaved and sawed open in Charlotte
yielded an egg-sized tumor.
The tracks where they backed across the yard
were still legible after the funeral

as the green seeped back into the stubble
over the cesspool.
That winter she had taken me to rake
leaves for cowbedding with a forked

stick in the woods above the barn.
I remember how naked the ground looked where
she gathered its cover into sacks,
and how the driver cursed the torn

roads over the mountain
when he slammed the spattered door
on her seventy years
of staying home.

— *Robert Morgan*

A Room in the Past

It's a kitchen. Its curtains fill
with a morning light so bright
you can't see beyond its windows
into the afternoon. A kitchen
falling through time with its things
in their places, the dishes jingling
up in the cupboard, the bucket
of drinking water rippled as if
a truck had just gone past, but that truck
was thirty years. No one's at home
in this room. Its counter is wiped,
and the dishrag hangs from its nail,
a dry leaf. In housedresses of mist,
blue aprons of rain, my grandmother
moved through this life like a ghost,
and when she had finished her years,
she put them all back in their places
and wiped out the sink, turning her back
on the rest of us, forever.

— *Ted Kooser*

Sundays Visiting

No one sat in the chair
even after she died.
It was hers and had arms
like a zoo animal is fat,
arms squeezed out of the sides
with the weight of its world
like her body, like the heavy
tips of her painful smile

and the edges of her eyes
and the bent corners
of the glasses that covered them
so thick I couldn't see in
and she couldn't see me.

But I could see the picture
above her everywhere, as if it
were hung in every room;
I don't remember if the picture
was framed; it was not of my
great-grandmother, but of Our Lady
of Fatima, of two eyes so black,
yet the eyes were not themselves
important, it was that color lacking
in them: steep, ragged black
straight back without discernible
borders or end or weight,
and under those eyes, uncommon,
shoe-black freckles, holes almost,
eaten through her face, pinpricks
showing flatly absent insides,
sucking me into the cramped space
of the thin picture like the sliding
edge of the bottomless well.

Such are the pictures of saints
which is what Fatima was, they said,
or better, perhaps angel, one of
the lower orders, but not a heavy
angel like the stories of Nijinsky
leaping; rather, an avenging angel
like the Mormon boy had told me,
with sword and surprise, each held
in a hand just out of the picture
waiting to catch a young boy
on a high toilet seat.

Her room was the last one
in back, the very small one
that fit her like a suit, always
locked, and whose windows
had been used elsewhere.

Behind the room was the canyon
where we went to throw rocks
as if that were our business,
to kick weeds, always hard,
to be outside the house.
Nothing hung in the air,
there was nowhere to sit
but on our thin heels, nothing
closed us in or locked us out
that we couldn't kick down
like weeds with our small feet,
the words of our new language.
From there, to the left, Mexico;
right, the weeds broken, two beer cans,
Tres Equis; ahead, houses on other hills
like barnacles seen in dry dock,
out of place, exposed, nowhere else
to go; and behind, the sound
of my cousin breathing obscenities
physically into the late summer wind,
September, October, whispering his words,
whispering to fool the wind
which always carries a secret farther.

—*Alberto Rios*

::

Grandpa's Picture

If the picture ever moved at all
there was no way we could tell:
the dust seemed just as thick
one year as the next
and Grandma never mentioned it;
so when one day a misthrown ball
caught a corner, spun the old frame
to the floor, we were appalled
at the sound she made and the flame
that rose in her face to burn
away the face that we had known.

No glass was broke and the frame was secure
when she placed it back on the desk,
but we never again were quite sure
of the meaning of the untouched dust
that coated his ancient sepia face
nor the unseen certain hand
that kept it in its place.

— Paul Ruffin

Daguerreotype of a Grandmother

    Is this the sum of her, or was she human?
When I unlatch the painted leather case
And slant the metal plate to show her face,
I catch the uncertain shadow of a woman
Standing inflexible, severe, undead.

What would the old photographer have said
In her excuse? She had to pose too long,
Staring in sunlight that was overstrong,
Until her gaze became forever set,
Her kindness marbled in austerity.
    So through the wire of a menagerie,
A farmyard fence, uneasy I have met
Just such an alien target-eye as she
Focuses uncommunicant on me.
    Now that the wise have ventured to uncere
Mummies in the museum, rays have flown
Clean through the wrappings to the crooked bone,
Splitting millenniums to make it clear
The young Egyptians could grow rickety
Without their vitamins as well as we.
    Let them anatomize the shadow here,
Whose body was not spiced nor honified.
Flyleaf of Bible hints how piously
She bore ten children, suffered for a year
From an affliction of the chest, and died.
    She shared our heritage and flexed our fate.
Now in her plushy border, hollow-eyed,
She is but ancestress, recalled today
As an unhappy shadow on a plate,
Burdened with love she cannot give away.

   — *Celeste Turner Wright*

Family Reunion

Sunlight glints off the chrome of many cars.
Cousins chatter like a flock of guineas.

In the shade of oaks and maples
six tables stand
filled with good things to eat.
Only the jars of iced tea sweat.

Here the living and dead mingle
like sun and shadow under old trees.

For the dead have come too,
those dark, stern departed who pose
all year in oval picture frames.

They are looking out of the eyes of children,
young sprouts
whose laughter blooms
fresh as the new flowers in the graveyard.

—Jim Wayne Miller

All

all he would have to say is,
remember the time I came home
with a beard and Dad didn't know me,
and we would all laugh,
Mom would say, just by your voice,
I knew your voice, and my sister
would say, the dog kept barking, and
I would say, that was the
summer I got a camera.
it pulls around us
like a drawstring, that time,
when we come together,
awkward and older,
our frayed conversations
trying to thread some memory
of each other,
one of us will only have to say,
remember the time you came home
from the bush with your beard,
and we were all easy again
with each other,
someone will say how
Mom knew his voice, someone
will remember how the dog barked, I
will remember my new camera,
and we are a family again,
young and laughing
on the front porch.

—*Leona Gom*

Acknowledgments

Permission to reprint copyrighted poems is gratefully acknowledged to the following:

Andrew Mountain Press, Hartford, CT, for "Cousin Ella Goes to Town" by George Ella Lyon, Copyright © 1983 by Andrew Mountain Press.

Atheneum Publishers, Inc., for "In the Motel" from *The Phantom Ice Cream Man: More Nonsense Poems* by X. J. Kennedy, Copyright © 1979 by X. J. Kennedy; A Margaret K. McElderry Book.

David B. Axelrod, for "Smell My Fingers" from *Home Remedies, New and Selected Poems* by David B. Axelrod (Cross-Cultural Communications, Merrick, NY), Copyright © 1984, 1982, 1976, 1974 by David B. Axelrod.

Robert Bly, for "At the Funeral of Great-Aunt Mary" from *Silence in the Snowy Fields* by Robert Bly (Wesleyan University Press, 1962), Copyright © 1961 by Robert Bly. Reprinted with his permission.

BOA Editions, Ltd., for "First Surf" from *Genesis* by Emanuel Di Pasquale, Copyright © 1983 by Emanuel Di Pasquale.

Borealis Press, Ltd., for "Great-Grandma" and "The New Mothers" from *Others* by Carol Shields.

Carnegie Mellon University Press, for "For My Daughter" and "Rowing" from *Miracle Mile* by Ed Ochester, Copyright © 1984 by Ed Ochester.

Siv Cedering, for "Poem for My Mother," Copyright © 1976, 1980 by Siv Cedering.

Clarke Irwin, Ltd., for "Helen's Scar" and "Subway Psalm" from *I Might Not Tell Everybody This* by Alden Nowlan, Copyright © 1983 by Clarke Irwin, Ltd., Copyright © 1982 by Alden Nowlan.

Vic Coccimiglio, for "Visit," Copyright © 1984 by Vic Coccimiglio.

Molly Malone Cook Literary Agency, Inc., for "A Letter from Home" from *No Voyage and Other Poems* by Mary Oliver, Copyright © 1965 by Mary Oliver.

Jill Dargeon, for "Buying the Dog" from *There's a Trick With a Knife I'm Learning to Do, Poems 1963-78* by Michael Ondaatje, Copyright © 1979 by Michael Ondaatje.

Delacorte Press/Seymour Lawrence, for "The Ascension: 1925" from

Koertge (Duck Down Press, 1976), Copyright © by Ronald Koertge.

Ted Kooser, for "A Room in the Past."

Greg Kuzma, for "For My Father on His Birthday" from *Good News* by Greg Kuzma, Copyright © 1973 by Greg Kuzma.

Little, Brown and Company, for "Poem for My Father's Ghost" from *Twelve Moons: Poems* by Mary Oliver, Copyright © 1976 by Mary Oliver (first appeared in *Prairie Schooner*); "My Father's Ghost" from *Landfall: Poems* by David Wagoner, Copyright © 1981 by David Wagoner.

Liveright Publishing Corporation, for "A Real Story" from *Aspects of Eve: Poems* by Linda Pastan, Copyright © 1970, 1971, 1972, 1973, 1974, 1975 by Linda Pastan.

Gerald Locklin, for "Poop" from *Poop and Other Poems* (Maelstrom Press, Cape Elizabeth, Maine), Copyright © 1972 by Gerald Locklin, Copyright © 1974 by Maelstrom Press (first appeared in *The Wormwood Review*, Mag and Maelstrom Press). Reprinted with the permission of the editor and author.

Lynx House Press, for "Stepfather: A Girl's Song" from *Lost in the Bonewheel Factory* by Yusef Komunyakaa, Copyright © 1979 by Yusef Komunyakaa.

George Ella Lyon, for "Birth" (first appeared in *Moving Out*) and "Catechisms: Talking with a Four-Year-Old" (first appeared in *Kentucky Poetry Review*).

Michigan Quarterly Review, for "Washing Windows" by Peter Wild (first appeared in *Michigan Quarterly Review, 20*, Fall 1981).

Jim Wayne Miller, for "Aunt Gladys's Home Movie No. 31, Albert's Funeral" and "Family Reunion" from *Dialogue with a Dead Man* (University of Georgia Press, Athens, 1974, reprinted by Green River Press, University of Michigan, 1978).

Robert Morgan, for "White Autumn" (first appeared in *Poetry*, September 1981), Copyright © 1981 by Modern Poetry Association. Reprinted with the permission of the editor of *Poetry* and the author.

Sheryl L. Nelms, for "Edwin A. Nelms" (previously published in *Lincoln Log, Nexus, Lutheran Women* and *National Poetry Press*), "How About" (previously published in *Confrontation, Kinverse Anthology, Up Against the Wall Mother* and *Broomstick*) and "Killing the Rooster" (previously published in *oakwood, Pteranodon, Embers, Horizons, Poetry Magazine, American Poetry Anthology* and *Princeton Sound and Fury*).

W. W. Norton & Company, Inc., for "Buying the Dog" from *There's a*

Mark Vinz, for "Business as Usual" (first appeared in *North American Review*, Summer 1976) and "Mac" (first appeared in *Northeast*, Winter 1981-82).

Valerie S. Warren, for "I Was the Child" (first appeared in *Intro #1*, ed. R. V. Cassill, Bantam Books, 1968).

Don Welch, for "The River," Copyright © 1983 by Don Welch.

Wesleyan University Press, for "The Dirty-Billed Freeze Footy," "My Mother's Death" and "We Interrupt This Broadcast" from *Very Close and Very Slow* by Judith Hemschemeyer, Copyright © 1975 by Judith Hemschemeyer; and "Sum" from *What Moves Is Not the Wind* by James Nolan, Copyright © 1980 by James Nolan, and "Mardi Gras/Grandmothers: Portrait in Red and Black Crayon" from *Why I Live in the Forest* by James Nolan, Copyright © 1974 by James Nolan.

Celeste Turner Wright, for "Daguerreotype of a Grandmother" from *Etruscan Princess and Other Poems* (Alan Swallow Press; first appeared in *The New Mexico Quarterly*), Copyright © 1964 by Celeste Turner Wright; "Murgatroyd" from *A Sense of Place* (Golden Quill Press), Copyright © 1973 by Celeste Turner Wright; and "The View from Father's Porch," Copyright © 1983 by Celeste Turner Wright.

Yet Another Small Magazine, for "Hunting at Dusk" by Doug Cockrell, Copyright © 1981 by Doug Cockrell.

Paul Zimmer, for "Missing the Children," Copyright © 1983 by Paul Zimmer.

Index of Poets

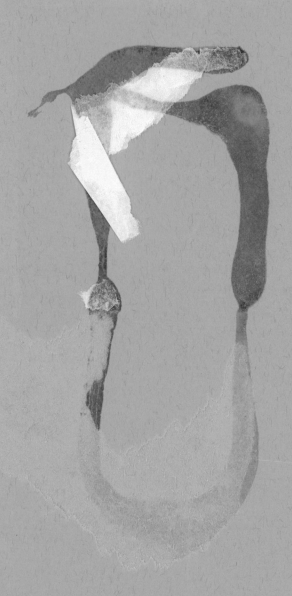